An Unforgettable Love

A CHRISTIAN HISTORICAL ROMANCE

SAGE CREEK

LORANA HOOPES

Copyright

Note from the Author

This book is dedicated to Christian Carufel, one of my Creative Writing students, who won the right to create a character. Christian Turner is the character he created and though some of this backstory doesn't appear in the book, here is his history:

He is a veteran of the Mexican-American War and the Civil War. Most of his life was spent in and around El Paso, having been a part of one of the first waves of settlers to the area. He was born in the Missouri Territory to a pair of corn farmers, went south to fight, and then moved back to try his hand at homesteading. During Bleeding Kansas, he moved to El Paso to hunt lizards. Eventually, he made a living manufacturing gunpowder for the local militias. During the Civil War, he was conscripted as part of the Texas Home Guard. He is stationed in Atlanta where his unit is almost wiped out by General Sherman and his army. He eventually moved back home where, affected by the war, he began to go crazy, seeing lights in the sky and moving mountains. He now spends his days wandering between his powder shack and the local drinking hole, and it is only a matter of time before he goes the way of all legends and explodes along with his powder trying to manufacture while heavily intoxicated.

I tried to stay true to the character and it was fun to add him in after most of the story was already plotted. He plays a big role though for a minor character.

Thank you so much for picking up this book. I hope you enjoy the story and the characters as they are dear to my heart. If you do, please leave a review at your retailer. It really does make a difference because it lets people make an informed decision about books.

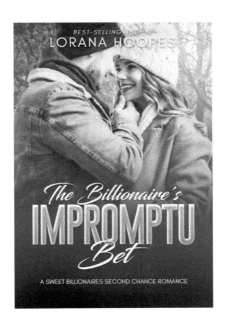

Sign up for Lorana Hoopes's newsletter and get her book, The Billionaire's Impromptu Bet, as a welcome gift. Get Started Now!

CHAPTER 1

Carl

Sage Creek, Texas 1884

Though the sun shone brightly in the clear Texas sky, it did nothing to calm the nerves constricting Carl Baxter's stomach as he approached the homestead of Jesse Jennings. It wasn't that he didn't know the man, but they weren't exactly close friends. Still, Jesse had information he needed. At least he hoped he did. Adjusting his hat, he took a deep breath to calm his nerves before lifting his hand and knocking at the door.

The door opened, but it was not Jesse on the other side. Instead his wife, Kate, stared at him, cradling a baby in her arms. "Can I help you?" she asked. Her tone was friendly but guarded which he understood. Though a local to the town, he hadn't spent much time around her and as she was friends with Emma Cook, he was sure she had heard stories about him. Stories that were probably less than flattering due to his behavior. He still cringed when he thought of how pushy he'd been.

He cleared his throat and removed his hat, twisting it in his hands and stifling the urge to run his fingers through his matted hair. Kate wouldn't care about his hair, but he also realized it was probably an unsightly mess after working all day, and he needed Kate to want to help him. "Yes, ma'am. I was hoping to speak to your husband. Is Jesse around?"

Kate tilted her head as she sized him up. The way her eyes raked over him made him feel as if she could see into the depths of his soul. Could she see his unease? She was a formidable woman for sure, and he understood more now how she had managed to escape the dangerous situation she found herself in when she first arrived in town. "He's out at the barn. Is something the matter?"

"Oh no, ma'am." His words spilled forth in a hurried tone to quell her fears. "I was just hoping to speak to him about a personal matter."

She stared at him for another moment as if weighing his words and his honesty. Then she nodded. "Very well." She pointed to a large red barn several yards away from the house. "You may find him there."

"Thank you, ma'am." He wished he knew Kate better so he could get a woman's perspective on his questions too, but that would not be proper to ask now. Perhaps he could have had Emma ask her… if he hadn't messed that situation up royally, and while she was conversing with him again, he wasn't sure he'd ever be able to mend their relationship completely.

Replacing his hat, he walked across the yard and stepped into the stifling heat of the barn. Though he could not see him at first, Carl followed the shuffling sound and found Jesse mucking a stall. Though in peak physical condition, sweat darkened the armpits of his shirt and rolled in rivulets down the side of his face. Carl cleared his throat so as not to startle the man. "Jesse? Can I have a word?"

Jesse paused and wiped a hand across his forehead. "What can I do for you, Carl?"

Carl cleared his throat again. This time in an attempt to push the words out that seemed lodged there like a dry biscuit. "I was wondering if I could ask you a few questions."

Jesse leaned against his rake and lifted a brow. It was clear he was curious what had brought Carl to his neck of the woods. "What about?"

Heat climbed up Carl's face. He couldn't believe he was about to ask this man he barely knew such intimate questions, but no one else had the insight he did. "About getting a mail-order bride. I know we don't know each other well, but as far as I know, you're the only one who has done it here, and I was hoping to get enough details to see if it's something I should consider."

Jesse's posture instantly relaxed and his hesitant expression slid into a friendly smile. "Well, I am certainly no expert. I didn't place the ad as I'm sure you know, but I did marry a woman I didn't know which I imagine is more what you're asking about. I'm happy to tell you what I can, but let's step outside where there's a little more air and a place to sit down." He leaned the rake against the side of the stall and led the way out of the barn.

Carl followed Jesse outside to where a small bench stood in the shade. The two men sat and then Jesse turned to him. "What is it you want to know?"

That was a very good question. Carl had thought about the questions he wanted to ask for the last few days, ever since he had accepted the fact that Emma was not going to give him a second chance. He looked down at his weathered and calloused hands, wondering if he even had enough to offer a woman. "I have many, but let's start with, is it worth it?"

Jesse nodded and ran a hand across his chin. "Well, I wasn't looking for a wife when Kate fell into my lap, but marrying her has been worth it. She's a wonderful woman."

"Was it difficult at first? Marrying a stranger?"

Jesse chuckled. "Marriage is always difficult, but having married the first time for love and the second time for convenience at first, I can say this marriage brought different challenges. It took time to get to know each other. With my first wife, we had courted before marriage, so we had plenty of opportunities to learn about each other. With Kate, I only knew her a short time before we married so we had to do the learning while we lived under the same roof. That part is different. It takes time."

Carl nodded. He had expected as much. It was one reason he had placed so much hope on marrying Emma. He'd known her forever. They'd grown up together. He knew they got along, and while he could tell she did not return the amorous feelings he had, he was sure they could have been happy. But he had no idea if he would get along with another woman and that was probably his biggest fear. "How long would you say it took?"

"A few weeks until we were comfortable. A few months before we realized love had sprouted. We were lucky in that area because I believe God blessed us." Jesse turned a discerning eye on Carl and lifted his eyebrow in question. "Have you prayed about this? Made sure it's His plan for you?"

Carl's eyes slid to the ground. He hadn't really prayed about this. Hadn't prayed about anything lately to be truthful. He'd been too angry at God for bringing William into Emma's life, but he knew Jesse was right and that he should pray about this. "Not as much as I should, but I will before I make a decision. I promise you."

"That's good. I understand the disappointment you must be feeling about Emma, but marriage is a lifelong commitment. Best not to jump into it lightly."

Carl sighed and placed his hands on his thighs. "I understand. Thank you for taking the time to answer my questions."

"You're welcome, but are you sure that is all you have?"

It wasn't, but the other questions swirling around in Carl's head were ones Jesse couldn't answer. How long would it take to find a woman? What would it cost? And what if he paid for the woman to come but she didn't? Or she did, but they couldn't get along? He wanted a family and he longed for companionship, but what if bringing a woman he didn't know into his life only brought misery and pain? With a sigh, he realized he better get right with God and begin praying because He was really the only one who could answer those questions.

"No, but you're right. Most of my other questions require God's answers." He thanked Jesse and shook his hand and then made his way back to his homestead. It was time to do something he'd been putting off for a while.

The sun had fully set by the time he finished removing the saddle and brushing his horse down, but Carl didn't mind. Evenings were generally his favorite time of the day as that was when his chores were done and he could sit and rest with his Bible in the evening. Of course, it had been a while since he'd been in the Bible. Lately, his evenings had been consumed with feeling sorry for himself and angry that William had come into Emma's life. Then he would retire to bed only to toss and turn for hours. Now, he realized that was probably due to his lack of peace over both his actions and his distance from his maker. Both things he would be remedying tonight.

After lighting his lantern and heating up some beans and cornbread - he was definitely looking forward to having someone to share supper with - he sat down at his table and opened his Bible. Unsure exactly what he was looking for, he simply opened the Bible, unsurprised to find himself reading about Ruth. She had the kind of devotion that he'd been lacking lately.

Before he could even finish his reading, he closed his eyes and prayed for forgiveness and for the answer to his question. Should he place an ad for a mail-order bride or did God have something different in mind for him?

CHAPTER 2

Elizabeth

Chicago 1884

Elizabeth Parker shivered as the chilly outside air bit through her light fabric. The weather had seemed brighter this morning when she'd left the house to check on her father, but now angry clouds darkened the sky and the temperature had dropped considerably. Enough that she wished she had a coat even though she wouldn't be outside long. Just long enough to run to the general store to look at the new shipment of fabric.

She couldn't buy any of course. There was no money for that, but she could look and she could dream. One day, she hoped to open a dress shop, even though she knew it was a lofty dream. Not only did most women sew their own clothing, but very few owned businesses. Still, times were changing, and it wasn't impossible. She'd heard rumors that a woman had opened a similar shop in Boston. None of that mattered though if her father didn't get better.

A rain drop pelted her face, and Elizabeth quickened her steps, but she wasn't fast enough. Moments later, the skies opened and rain poured down. By the time she reached the general store, she was soaked to the bone. Margaret, the store owner's wife glanced up as she entered, and concern etched itself in every line of her face.

"Elizabeth, are you okay?"

"Fine." Elizabeth brushed her shoulders in an effort to remove the water, but it was useless. The two had merged into one cold and heavy conglomeration. "Just didn't expect it to rain today."

"It's raining?" Margaret stepped closer to the window and shook her head. "Normally, my ankle tells me when rain is coming, but I didn't feel anything today."

Elizabeth wasn't sure of Margaret's exact age, but her dark hair held only a few strands of gray and her face only the slightest trace of fine lines that seemed much more prominent with age, so Elizabeth doubted she was that much older. Still, she claimed that her ankle, which she'd broken when she was young, could predict the weather. Evidently, it ached more when rain was coming, and for the most part, Margaret was correct.

"It seemed to come out of nowhere today," Elizabeth agreed as she made her way over to the fabrics. "I hope that doesn't mean we're in for a short summer."

Margaret sighed and joined her at the fabric display. "Me too. I just ordered some new lighter fabrics. I'd hate for them not to be bought."

"Oh, I wish I could get them when they come in. I could

use a new summer dress." Elizabeth allowed herself to dream as she ran her fingers over a pretty checkered fabric. This one would be lovely for picnics and church outings and could be elevated with a lace collar and a touch of lace on the sleeves.

"Well, if you promise not to tell Brian," Margaret looked around conspiratorially for her husband who owned the store, "I might be able to trade some fabric in exchange for a dress. I can sew, but I rarely have time, and yours always look so much better than mine."

Elizabeth smiled at her friend. "Your dresses are lovely, Margaret, but if you're serious, I will take you up on that offer. With Pa being sick, it might be the only way I can afford it."

Margaret's smile faltered. "I'm so sorry to hear about your father. I sure hope he recovers."

"Thank you. Me too, but I'm trying not to focus on it right now which is why I'm here looking at your beautiful fabric. Tell me about this one," Elizabeth said, hoping to change the subject and lighten the mood.

Margaret's smile returned as she talked about the lovely silk fabric that Elizabeth held. Silk was too expensive to make an entire dress out of, but Elizabeth loved to use it as an accessory piece when she could. The women talked a little longer, sharing ideas for dresses and recipes until a harried voice grabbed Elizabeth's attention.

"Miss Parker?"

The two women turned toward the door, and when Elizabeth saw who it was, her heart sank. She'd left instructions for the nurse to come and retrieve her if her father's condition worsened, so her appearance meant nothing good.

"It's your father, Miss Parker. I think you'll want to come back."

Elizabeth nodded and let her hand fall from the fabric. It was silly to dream anyway. With her mother gone and her father's health waning, there would be no way she'd ever be able to buy new fabric, much less start a dressmaking business. Not unless she married a wealthy man, and with her independent streak that seemed highly unlikely.

"I'm sorry, Margaret, I have to go."

Margaret shook her head. "Of course. I hope everything is alright."

It wasn't, but Elizabeth merely flashed a small smile and then followed the nurse back out into the rain. It was coming down harder now, and the clouds had taken on a dark, menacing appearance, one that sent chills through Elizabeth's spine.

The nurse entered the clinic first, but Elizabeth was right on her heels and rushed to her father's side. She gripped his hand and startled at how much worse he looked. It had barely been an hour if that, but all the color was gone from his complexion. His hand was cold, and though she had long wished she could heal him, holding his hand now felt cold and clammy as if life had already left it. He'd been fighting the illness for weeks, and she had known that the end was near, but he was all she had left, and she had no idea what she would do when he was gone.

"Pa, please don't die on me. I don't know what I'm going

to do without you." She picked up a nearby towel with her free hand and wiped the beads of sweat from his forehead.

His eyes flicked open, but only briefly. "I took care of that," he said, his voice raspy, his chest heaving as he struggled to breathe.

A cold sensation gripped her heart. "Took care of it? How? What do you mean?"

"Jacob Canfield will watch after you."

"Jacob Canfield? The owner of the saloon?" She did not know the man well, but her father had befriended him in the last several years. After her mother's death, the saloon had become a safe haven for her father, a place for him to drink away his sorrow and wallow in his pity. She had never approved, but while she'd voiced her opposition and prayed continually about it, it had not been enough to dissuade him from the frequent visits. However, she had not known her father was close enough with the sleazy other man to ask him to look out for her when he passed. "You cannot leave me with Jacob Canfield."

"He's a good man," her father wheezed, each word halting and labored.

Elizabeth had her doubts about that, but she decided to try a different line of reasoning. "But he owns a saloon. What if he asks me to work there? You would not want that for me, would you, Pa?"

With the little strength he had, her father shook his head. "He won't. We have worked out an agreement. He is only to watch after you."

Elizabeth had no doubt Jacob had promised her father

that, but she also had little doubt that he would follow that promise. Granted, she was making assumptions, but every fiber in her body told her that he could not be trusted. However, her father was dying and she would not fill his final moments with arguments. She would find a way to take care of herself and trust that God would provide for her.

"Okay, Pa. I will trust you, but please fight. If you fight a little more, you can beat this. I know you can." The deathly pallor emanating from him told her the exact opposite, but the words made her feel better, and she hoped they would bring relief to her father as well.

"I am too tired to keep fighting, but I will be with Jesus soon. I hate that I am leaving you here, but I do not want you to worry about me. I will be fine."

Tears blurred her vision as she squeezed his hand a little tighter. "I know you will, Pa, and you will get to see Ma and Abigail again." Her mother had died years before during childbirth with her little sister Abigail who never got to take her first breath in this world before she was whisked away to Heaven.

"Yes, I can almost see them now." Her father's voice was weaker, almost distant, as if he really was almost at Heaven's door and no longer in the room with her. "It is beautiful." For a moment, a smile lit up his face, and Elizabeth felt a glimmer of hope that maybe God was healing him and would send him back, but then the smile froze. There was a final rugged breath and then her father was still.

"No, Pa." Even though she knew that it was useless, she

shook him, hoping to bring him back, to flood life into his veins once again, but it was not to be. He remained still, the smile etched onto his face and his eyes focused on something far away.

"He's gone, my dear, I'm sorry." The nurse, who had been watching from the corner of the room to give them privacy, stepped forward and closed her father's eyes with her hand. "There is nothing more we can do."

Elizabeth sniffed and dabbed at her eyes. Every bone in her body longed to crumple into the corner and remain there until she too passed away, but she knew that she could not do that. She would have to be stronger now. She would have to find a way to take care of herself, and she would need God now more than ever. Her faith had been shaken over the last few years, but her mother's voice reminding her that God loved her and was always in control, even when it seemed darkest, kept her devotion from wavering.

"Do you have someone to take you home?" the doctor asked, stepping into the room. He was an older gentleman, with graying hair and weathered features, but he had been nothing but gentle with her, and his kindness reverberated in his voice.

Home. Did she even know where that was now? Did she go back to the house she had shared with her father? It was all she knew, but she was also aware that she did not have money to keep making the payments. How long would the bank allow her to remain before they came and took it all away? She would have to find a job, some way to earn enough money to remain in the house or find a smaller place that she could afford.

"I will be fine," she said, pulling back her shoulders, "my house isn't far." Although she had no intention of going straight there. A stop in every available store that might afford employment would happen first.

The doctor nodded and placed a hand on her shoulder. It was a fatherly gesture and did not give her discomfort. "I will make sure the body is taken care of and have the minister reach out to you about funeral arrangements."

Elizabeth nodded. She had not even thought about a funeral, but she supposed it would be necessary. "Thank you."

She stepped out of the doctor's office and into the bright sunlight, blinking against the blinding light. It had been pouring only moments ago when she'd returned to the clinic and now it was sunny? It was like a bad joke, and she felt a glimmer of anger spark in her chest. How could it be so cheery outside when she felt like she was dying inside? How could God send sunshine when her entire world had just fallen apart?

"Is he gone then?"

Elizabeth turned to the voice, jumping back at the sight of Jacob Canfield leaning against the column. Bile burned the back of her throat at the mere sight of him, and her anger grew but this time it was at the man in front of her and not God. "What are you doing here?"

His lips pulled into a shape that she suspected was meant to be a smile but looked more like a lion about to devour prey. "I'm here to pay my respects, of course."

His respects? That was rich. She doubted he had respect for anything. "I'm afraid you're too late then."

He chuckled, a low mirthless sound that sent shivers running down Elizabeth's spine. "No, I'm right on time. Paying my respects was only part of the reason I came. The other reason is to collect my property."

"Property? What property?"

"You." He was a large man. His shirt and jacket strained the buttons and his face was thick and fleshy, but it was his eyes that filled her with dread. They were cold and dark and intimidating.

She would not let him know he intimidated her though. Elizabeth threw her shoulders back, standing as straight as she could manage. "I am not property and will be going nowhere with you. My father may have made an agreement with you to watch out for me, but I was not consulted."

Jacob pushed off the column, an expression of anger darkening his features. "You didn't need to be consulted. It was a business transaction between men and not a woman's affair."

The anger within her grew. She knew that many men thought like Jacob did - that women were too dumb to understand business - but this was even worse. He believed she was property to be owned, and she was having a hard time seeing him as a fellow creation. "I am not a business transaction. My father may not have realized, but I am capable of taking care of myself and that is what I will be doing." She turned to head in the opposite direction, but Jacob caught up to her and pulled on her arm, forcing her to turn back to him.

"You will come with me because that was the deal."

She tried to shake his hand from her arm, but it was no use. He was stronger than she was, and his fingers dug into her arm through the fabric of her dress like talons. She had no doubt there would be bruises there tomorrow. "No, the deal my father told me was that you watch out for me. Nothing more. Now, please remove your hand from my arm." Noticing the nearby people in the street, Elizabeth raised her voice to draw attention to the situation.

Dark clouds formed in Jacob's eyes, but after glancing at the crowd stopping to stare, he dropped her arm. His voice was loud enough for her only to hear as he whispered. "You will be mine and there is nothing you can do about it. I'll see you later." Then he flashed a malicious smile at her and left.

Elizabeth leaned against the wall of the clinic and breathed. "Lord, thank you for the protection, but I'm going to need help here," she whispered. She had bought herself a little time, but she was afraid that Jacob might turn out to be right. If she couldn't find a way to support herself, there would be little else she could do. Women had few options in society, especially if they were unmarried and without family, but she would not go down without a fight. When

she was sure that Jacob was gone and would not be returning, she made her way back to the general store. She knew
Margaret wasn't hiring, but she carried the newspaper there,
and she hoped it might give her options for employment.

CHAPTER 3
Elizabeth

Elizabeth sighed as she sank into the chair. Her feet throbbed and her spirit was low. There had been no advertisements looking to hire women in the paper and none of the reputable places were in need of someone at the moment either. That left only two options. She could go to work for Jacob, the thought of which repulsed her to her very core, or she could answer the mail-order bride request she had seen in the paper. Marriage had never been something she had seen for herself. Not that she didn't want to get married, but most men saw her as too independent, and moving out west had certainly never crossed her mind before now, but marriage to a stranger had to be better than working for Jacob.

"Please, Lord, show me what You want for me. Help me to know what to do." She pressed her fingers to her forehead, trying to drown out the inner voice whispering to her that God wasn't real, that He couldn't hear her prayers, that He didn't care about her.

The voice had started when she was young, when her mother died, but her mother had been a strong woman of faith and she had planted seeds that had been watered for years in Elizabeth's mind. Those seeds had grown strong enough before her mother's death that they were able to withstand the whispered urgings of the voice trying to pull her from God. Elizabeth had become the woman of faith in her house and made sure her father continued to take her to church every Sunday. The voice had quieted, but there had been days when it would whisper that she needed a husband or that her prayers were being wasted on her father. And then her father had gotten sick. Elizabeth had tried to remain strong, but the voice had gotten louder, and now with her father gone, with everything gone, it threatened to choke out the truth that Elizabeth knew, the words she held onto from her mother.

The pounding of a knock at her door caused Elizabeth to jump, and she quickly closed the paper before rising to see who was at the door. Most likely it was a neighbor who had heard about her father's death and wanted to convey their condolences. She wasn't really in the mood for that, but she tried to put on her best smile. However, it faded as soon as she opened the door and saw Jacob and another man standing there. Elizabeth could not believe the nerve of this man showing up here after she'd already told him she was not property. Couldn't he at least give her a day to grieve? How had her father ever called this man a friend?

"What do you want?" she asked, folding her arms across her chest to create a barrier. "I already told you I'm not property."

Jacob smiled at her, but it was a sinister smile, one that sent a trail of ice down her back all the way to her toes. "I guess he forgot to tell you he put our agreement in writing."

"What?" Elizabeth's eyes narrowed as a feeling of fear crawled up her neck. "He would do no such thing."

"I guess you didn't know him as well as I did," Jacob said, pulling a piece of paper from his pocket and holding it out for her. "He signed this just two days ago."

Elizabeth took the paper and glanced down to the bottom. Sure enough her father's signature was there, but why would he??? She lifted her eyes to begin reading the paper, but before she could, Jacob ripped it out of her hands.

"You saw his signature, I'm sure," Jacob said, folding the paper up and tucking it back into his pocket.

Elizabeth glared up at him. "I saw a signature, but I have no idea what the paper said as you didn't give me time to read it, and even if that was my father's signature, he was barely conscious the last few days. He would have had no idea what he was signing."

Jacob shrugged. "Maybe it was during his lucid moments. Either way, it doesn't matter. You belong to me."

"I might have to work for you, but I do not belong to you. I am not property."

Jacob's fleshy lips pulled into a grin and she tried not to be disgusted by the line of spittle she saw hanging from the corners. "We can quibble over the details later, but right now, you will gather your things and then you will be accompanying me to the saloon. There are rooms upstairs and you will set up there."

Elizabeth clenched her hands into fists. She knew exactly what those rooms upstairs were normally used for and if he thought she was going to participate in that trade, he had another thing coming. Working in the saloon would be bad enough, but she was not going to prostitute herself. She would run away before it ever came to that.

Her mind drifted back to her prayer and the newspaper, and she forced herself not to let her eyes follow. Was that God's will then? She'd asked for answers, and the advertisement in that paper might very well hold her key for getting away from Jacob. There was nothing keeping her here any longer. Her father had been the last of her family and with no chance to take another reputable job, there was no employment keeping her here either. The only question was would out west be far enough or would Jacob look for her even there?

It would be ridiculous for him to try and come after her - she wasn't worth the money he'd spend, but Jacob was stubborn and if he really saw her as his property, he might. Still, it was probably her only shot.

She knew little about the west, but she imagined it was not as advanced as Chicago. Still, with a new name and a husband, she would be able to find a place to blend in and elude Jacob's far reach. With her plan settled in her mind, she lifted her chin and stared into Jacob's eyes.

"Fine, but there will be rules. I will work at the saloon as a server and nothing more, and I must have time to myself."

Jacob chuckled and shook his head. "You are in no position to be making demands."

"And you are in no position to make me property. Whatever that paper says, I doubt any court would agree that you have complete ownership over me. My father said you were to watch over me. That is all. What do you think will hold more weight? A paper signed by a delirious man or a deathbed confession to his only daughter?"

The muscles in Jacob's neck tensed and Elizabeth could tell he hadn't thought that part through. No doubt the paper barely said anything and he had just been hoping to get her to agree through sheer bruteness, but she was not a woman to be pushed around like that. Her fierce independent streak might be why she was not married yet, but it had also saved her more than once.

"Fine," he said, shaking his head. "We will work out the details later."

Elizabeth knew there was little chance he would work anything out with her, but she hoped she had bought herself some time at least. She had no idea how long it might take to reach out to the man in the west, but she knew she needed to move quickly and yet without arousing Jacob's suspicions.

"What is going to happen to my family's things?" she asked, glancing back over her shoulder. There weren't a ton of heirlooms - a lot had already been sold after her mother died - but there were things she wanted to keep.

"That's where I come in," the man with Jacob said,

speaking up for the first time. He was not a small man, but his face was so pinched and tight and he curled in on himself so much that he reminded Elizabeth of an owl. Even his voice held a screechy tone. "My name is Mr. Stevens. I represent the bank. Your father left strict instructions that the bedding and the dishes were to be boxed up and kept for you until you married, but I'm afraid everything else belongs to the bank."

"Everything?" Elizabeth looked at the chair her mother had often rocked in, the one she had hoped to rock her own child in one day.

"I'm afraid so. With no way to pay the mortgage, it defaults to the bank. We have to repossess it."

Elizabeth swallowed the emotion welling in her throat. "Very well. Please give me some time to pack my things." Though she knew it was rude, she shut the door on them before they could say anything else. She might have to leave her home, but she wasn't going to give them the satisfaction of seeing her emotional about it.

Grabbing a bag from the closet, she began to pack her dresses and other clothes. She grabbed her Bible from the table and then looked about her room. It was the only room she'd known her entire life, but there was little here that she could take with her.

She carried the bag into the kitchen and stood still for a moment as she scanned the room. What did she want to take? For so long, it had just been her and her father, but if she was to leave this place forever, she wanted something to remember her parents by. Her eyes fell to the table and her father's mug. The one he drank his coffee in every morning. She tucked it into her bag and then grabbed her mother's knitting needles from the basket by the chair and added them too. The knitting instruments were about the only thing she had left of her mother's that hadn't been sold already, besides the locket she wore around her neck, and Elizabeth would need knitting needles anyway. She looked over the room once more. There was so much history here. How could she leave it all?

Knuckles rapped at the door again, and Jacob's impatient voice carried through the door. "Are you ready?"

"Almost." She scooped up the newspaper and then hurried into her father's room and pulled the quilt from the bed. It had been a gift to her mother at their wedding, and though she would never have anyone to give her such a thing, she could take this one and imagine that her mother would have given it to her on her wedding day.

With her arms full, she returned to the entryway and opened the door. Both men still stood there, the banker looking even more uncomfortable than before and Jacob reminding her of a bull ready to charge.

"What took you so long?" he snarled.

She lifted her chin at him. "I'm leaving the only home I've ever known and have no idea what is going to happen to the rest of the items. I was packing what I needed and saying goodbye."

"Fine, but we need to get going. I have a business to run after all."

She lifted her chin in defiance. "Well, you could just stay

there and leave me out of your business."

He let out a mirthless chuckle and shook his head. "'Fraid not. I've already got a dress with your name on it."

Elizabeth clenched her jaw to keep from emitting a sarcastic remark. She had no desire to wear a dress that some other woman had worn before her, especially considering the type of women he employed. Though she supposed she fell into that category now herself. But not for long. She would answer that ad in the newspaper and get out of this town. Anything would be better than working for Jacob.

"The house is all yours," Jacob said to the banker before taking Elizabeth by the elbow and leading her to his wagon. Even this impersonal touch sent shivers down her spine and she shook her arm free.

"I would advise you not to touch me. I am a lady and I will not be soiled by the likes of you."

Jacob laughed again and shook his head, but he removed his hand and didn't touch her again until offering a hand to help her up into the wagon. She ignored his offer and instead lifted her skirts slightly and pulled herself into the front of the wagon. It was a small thing, but she would do anything to avoid his touch.

There was a gleam in his eye as he walked around to the other side and took the reins. He was enjoying this, and she had no doubt he would enjoy trying to break her spirit, but she would not give him the chance. The first chance she got, she would be returning to the store and sending a message back to Mr. Baxter. She would not stay here.

CHAPTER 4

Elizabeth

"What do you think you are doing, girl? Are you so hopeless that you can't even get the drinks to the right table?"

Elizabeth bit the inside of her lip to keep from yelling back at Luther, the bartender. With his long wavy hair and cold as ice eyes, he was the one person who gave her pause. He'd never hit her, but she'd seen him beat some of the other women. She'd also seen him break up bar fights between men twice his size which probably explained the many scars that marred his face. At one point, he could have been considered handsome, but his brutality distorted any remnants of compassion on his features.

"I'm sorry." She hated apologizing to him, but it was only for a time she reminded herself. She'd already written a response back to the farmer in Texas and if everything went well, she'd be able to sneak out and mail it today.

"Don't worry about him. He's especially grumpy today because some of his alcohol was looted last night."

Mary kept her voice low, but Elizabeth appreciated the kind words even if they were quiet. Mary was one of the older women and she'd worked for Jacob for years. Her face showed signs of abuse and she limped a little when she walked, but somehow she managed to keep a positive spirit and encourage the other women.

"Thank you. I can't imagine who would be dumb enough to steal from him though."

Mary nodded and glanced around. "Even worse. They think it was an inside job because no one broke in."

Elizabeth's eyes widened. Someone on the inside had turned on the formidable bartender? No wonder he was in a bad mood. "I guess I better pay extra attention today then. If he is on a warpath, I have no desire to get in his way."

"Nor do I." Mary flashed a smile before moving to the opposite side of the saloon to help her customers.

The saloon was not quite as busy as it would be later in the evening, but there were still enough patrons that three girls were needed on the floor. Elizabeth had the crowd to the right, Mary had the crowd to the left, and Bess had the crowd in the middle. Bess was one of the women that Elizabeth tried her hardest to avoid. As soon as she'd showed up, Bess had made it her mission to be as rude and snide to Elizabeth as possible.

"Ladies, I'd like to introduce you to our newest girl, Elizabeth Parker," Jacob said, pushing her forward like she was a horse on display.

Most of the girls offered small smiles and quiet hellos, but one lady stepped forward, her facial features twisted into an angry grimace. "You think you're better than us, don't you?"

Elizabeth opened her mouth to reply and then thought better of it. It wasn't that she thought she was better than the women - it was obvious some of them had lived a hard life - but she did feel she was better than working in an establishment such as this. Still, she could tell from Bess's chiseled gaze that stating so out loud would not be a good idea. Plus, she had a suspicion that some of Bess's hostility was related to the fact that she was a larger woman and probably didn't get the same ogling looks the other women received. Not that Elizabeth enjoyed those looks in any way. She decided to try and offer an olive branch. "No, I simply had not planned for this to be my life."

Bess snorted and rolled her eyes. "You think any of us chose this as our plan for our life? That's rich, honey. We all got thrown into this just like you, so you can step off your high horse and realize you're now one of us. One of the untouchables."

The saloon women weren't untouchable per say, but decent women in society did not generally associate with them. Their companions were either each other or the rough men who frequented the saloon which made for a pretty lonely existence.

Not for long, Elizabeth thought, but anytime in this place was too long and the snail's pace at which the mail moved made it even longer, but she was determined this would not be her end.

"Watch where you're going," Bess said as she deliberately bumped into Elizabeth. The amber liquid in the glasses on her tray sloshed to one side and then the next, but Elizabeth managed to counter the effect and keep the beer from spilling. She shot a glare at Bess who merely smiled and sashayed back to her side before placing the beers on the table in front of the men.

"That was a neat balancing act," one of them said as his eyes traveled from her face down to her waist. "I bet you have a few other tricks that would be worth exploring." His hand snaked out to snag her arm.

Revulsion shot through Elizabeth, and she fought the urge to smack the man's hand away. "I'm afraid I'm not your girl for that, and I am going to ask you to kindly remove your hand from my person."

"Oh, you're going to ask me kindly, huh?" He grinned at the man across from him, revealing a row of brown teeth. "What do you think, Clyde? Should I let her go? She asked me kindly."

Clyde leaned back in his chair and scanned Elizabeth's form as well. His face was rugged and scarred, but his eyes were like pieces of coal after the fire had burned out. They were cold and lifeless. "I think that sounded more like an invitation to me."

"I think you might be right."

Before Elizabeth could react, the man snapped her to him and she found herself on his lap, his breath heavy with alcohol and the stench of rotting teeth.

"Where I come from," he whispered in her ear, "women know their place and don't talk back to men."

Repulsion flooded her body, but Elizabeth knew that she couldn't let it paralyze her, so instead, she turned to look at the man and tried to put on her bravest air. "Where I come from, men respect women and know when their touch is unwanted. Now, I have a job to do and unless you want the bartender, who is having a very bad day, to come over, I suggest you let me do my job."

The man sneered at her. "You think I'm scared of your bartender?"

Across the table, Elizabeth saw Clyde's eyes widen and a moment later, she felt Luther's firm grip on the shoulder of the man holding her. "You should be. Now get your hands off my girl before I remove them myself."

While Elizabeth did not appreciate being called "his girl," she could not deny the feeling of relief when the man let go of her and she was able to distance herself from his stench and his filth.

"Go get some air," Luther said, pointing to the door, "but be back before the next rush."

Elizabeth nodded, grateful for the reprieve and the chance to swing by the post office to drop off her letter. Now more than ever, she wanted to escape this place.

As soon as she stepped into the fresh air, Elizabeth felt as if a burden had been lifted from her shoulders. It was amazing how oppressing the dark saloon was even though Luther generally did a good job keeping men from touching her. She took a moment to let the sun shine down on her face before she continued to the general store.

Her old friend Margaret looked up as she entered, but then her eyes dropped. There would be no chatter of dresses or fabric today. She could no longer look Elizabeth in the eye. Nor could many of the other women Elizabeth had known.

Elizabeth, determined not to let the other woman's actions affect her, pulled back her shoulders and marched to the counter. "I'd like to mail this," she said, pulling the letter out of her pocket where she'd kept it for such a moment as this.

Margaret took the envelope, but her eyes remained focused down. "Very well." She flipped it over and scanned the details. Then her eyes flicked up briefly. "Texas? Do you have family there?"

A week ago, Elizabeth would have told her everything, but she didn't know if she could trust Margaret now. She didn't know if she could trust anybody. "How much please?"

Margaret nodded and gave her the total. Elizabeth fished the money out of her pocket and handed it over. "How long will it take, do you think?"

"At least a week to make it there and get a response," Margaret said.

A week. She had known it would take at least that long, but it still felt like forever. How on earth would she survive another grueling week in the saloon? "Very well. I'll check back then."

She turned to leave, but Margaret called out to her. "Elizabeth? I'm sorry..."

Elizabeth nodded, but she did not turn around. Margaret might once have been a friend, but she no longer was, and Elizabeth had no time to dwell in the past. She had to focus on the future and getting out of Chicago.

CHAPTER 5

Carl

Carl stared at the letter in his hands. He couldn't believe she had actually written him back. After speaking with Jesse and spending a few days in prayer, he'd felt that God was sending him in this direction, so he'd scoured the newspaper for ads from women looking to head west. Nothing had grabbed his attention, so he'd placed his own.

"Thirty year old farmer looking for good Christian woman to marry and help with house." It had been simple, too simple he'd worried, but now he had a letter in his hand. A response from a woman in Chicago named Elizabeth Parker.

"Thank you," he said to Mr. Brown, who served as both the general store owner and the mail clerk for the town, before tucking the letter in his pocket. He'd read it but not here. He wanted to go somewhere away from curious eyes. He found a bench around the side and sat down. The soft light of the afternoon sun and the lingering warmth in the air seemed to add a perfect touch to the situation.

He opened the envelope and pulled out the folded paper, blinking as a soft flowery scent accompanied it. Had she put perfume on the paper and if so, why? Perhaps her words would explain. He unfolded the paper and stared at the feminine script. Clearly she was educated or else she'd had someone who was educated write the letter for her. He supposed that was possible, but if she lived in Chicago, perhaps she had more access to schooling than girls did out here. Schools were becoming more popular but most girls never finished.

That thought gave him pause. If she was educated, why would she want to move out west? And could she be happy if she couldn't use her education out here? Did she perhaps think he would be able to offer her a better life? Maybe he should have explained that he had little. His family was all gone, he had a small house, and he worked hard. He considered it a good life, but it was a simple one for sure. Would it be enough for her? He sighed and began to peruse the words. There was only one way to find out.

"Dear Mr. Baxter, My name is Elizabeth Parker and I live in Chicago. My father recently passed away and I am looking for a new start in life. I have no family here to tie me to Chicago any longer and believe the west may hold a new adventure for me. I am a Christian woman and though I am unfamiliar with farming, I am good at keeping house. I have been in charge of keeping my father's house since my mother died. Please let me know at your earliest convenience if you find me agreeable as I would like to leave Chicago as soon as possible. Elizabeth."

Well, that answered a few questions. If she had no family back home, then she might care less about putting her education to good use, and it meant that she would probably stay as there was nothing to draw her back to Chicago. He'd heard rumors of some men paying for a woman to come out west, only to have her decide a few months later she would rather return home. Money was too scarce to be spent so frivolously.

Still, there was little about the woman herself. Yes, she appeared eager to move away from Chicago, but was she too eager? The death of her father could certainly be a reason, if it was true, but how could he tell for sure? She'd said she was a Christian woman but nothing about church. Did she not attend in Chicago? Maybe the two were synonymous to her which was why she hadn't clarified. But was this the right move? Was she the right woman?

Sighing, he tucked the letter into his pocket and made his way back to his horse. Christian Turner leaned against the general store railing mumbling to himself, but Carl paid him little mind as he climbed into the saddle. The man had arrived a few months ago claiming he was a prospector out to find gold, but he seemed to spend more time talking to himself than looking for the precious metal. At first, he'd raised some eyebrows, but now everyone in town had just accepted that he might be a little light in the head. Sometimes, Carl would take a few minutes to have a conversation with the man, but it was getting late today, and it was high time he returned to his homestead and finished his chores. Then, he could spend time asking God if Elizabeth was the right woman before he responded.

When he arrived at his cabin, he read the letter one more time and then set it on the table to peruse again over dinner. He sent up a prayer for wisdom and then headed out to complete his work for the day.

When the sun sank low on the horizon, sending purples and reds streaking across the sky, he put his horse up for the night and returned to his kitchen. It was cold and dark and he wished again that he had a woman who could make the room feel brighter and have a meal ready when he returned. Could Elizabeth be that woman? His eyes fell to the letter once again as he cut off a slice of bread and chewed to calm the hunger in his stomach. He'd prayed the whole time he was working, but there had been no gut feeling one way or the other and Carl wasn't sure what that meant.

Perhaps it meant that God approved since he didn't get a negative feeling about the proposal, but he had hoped for a stronger sign that this was God's will. Still, perhaps the fact that he couldn't stop thinking about the woman who wrote the letter was his sign.

Decided, he grabbed a piece of stationary from the table and began to write a response to Elizabeth.

Dear Miss Parker,

I am sorry to hear about your father.

Carl paused and tapped the pencil against his lips. This was it. If he wrote to her that he'd like her to come west, he really couldn't change his mind. It wouldn't be fair to her, and he couldn't really just send another letter trying to get to know her. The time it took for a letter to travel and get a response was too long. She might change her mind by then. He closed his eyes and prayed again, only this time he made it more about her. He asked for clarity on whether offering her a ticket would be the right thing for her and when he felt a strong sense of urgency that she needed out of Chicago, that was enough for him. Opening his eyes, he finished the letter.

But I am pleased that you wrote to me. I am enclosing a ticket to make the journey and look forward to meeting you soon.

The letter was short, but there was little else he could say, especially not knowing the woman. All he could do was pray this was the right decision. He folded the letter and moved it to the side before placing the leftover beef and beans from dinner on the stove to warm it for supper. He had once enjoyed beef and beans, but when it became his meal two to three times a day, it quickly lost its appeal. Even if Elizabeth wasn't a great cook, any variety she could bring would be appreciated.

When the food was warmed enough, he sat back at the table and began to eat. Like it always did, the silence began to creep in on him, reminding him how very lonely he was. His eyes shifted to the letter. It was the right move. He was sure of it. If she agreed to come, at least he would have someone to talk to in the evenings and that would make it all worth it.

CHAPTER 6
Elizabeth

Elizabeth could not contain her excitement as she raced out of the general store with the ticket in her hand. It had taken ten days, ten long grueling days, but finally she had received not only word from Mr. Baxter, but also a ticket which meant she could be out of here tomorrow at the very latest. Maybe she would even get lucky and there would be a train leaving tonight.

She tucked the ticket in her pocket and ran towards the train station, hoping that she could get there and back to the saloon before she was missed. It was her afternoon off, but no girl got the evening off, and if she wasn't back before the start of shift, she would be in trouble. She didn't want Jacob getting wind of her plan before she was gone.

"Please, is there a train to Texas today?" she asked, her words halting as she tried to catch her breath.

The man behind the booth raised his eyebrows at her. "We do have one train leaving in an hour."

An hour. Would it be enough time? Could she make it to her room, pack, and disappear without being seen in that time? She would have to. There was no way she could wait until tomorrow. She had a feeling that if she did, something would keep her from being able to leave.

"I'll take it. Thank you." She handed the open ticket to the clerk in exchange for the scheduled ticket and looked toward the bustling platform. "Where will I go to catch the train?"

"This train will depart from platform two just over there." The clerk pointed, and following his finger, Elizabeth saw small square boxes with numbers hanging from the ceiling. Number two was on the far side.

"Thank you." She tucked the ticket he extended her into her pocket and then made her way back toward the saloon. Sneaking in the back entrance, she climbed the stairs quietly, stepping over the nasty fourth step that always groaned when you stepped on it, and then threw as many items as she could into her bag. There would be things left behind, but she couldn't think about them now. Items could be replaced. All that mattered now was getting out of here while she could.

"Are you going somewhere?"

Elizabeth glanced up to see Mary standing in her doorway. She bit the inside of her lip. Mary had always been nice to her, but could she trust her? The woman didn't look angry, merely curious, so deciding she didn't have much of an option, Elizabeth issued a silent prayer that Mary wouldn't turn her in or at least not until she could get on the train and answered. "I am. I can't stay here. This was never what my father planned for me, so I'm leaving town."

Mary's brow lifted slightly. "Where will you go?"

Elizabeth shook her head. "I don't know exactly. I'm going to let it be an adventure." That wasn't exactly true - she had the name of where she was going - but even though she was fairly certain Mary wouldn't squeal on her, she wanted to protect her from having any concrete information she could share.

For a second, Mary just stared at her and Elizabeth was sure the woman was going to block the door and holler for Luther, but finally she smiled, stepped in to give Elizabeth a hug, and wished her luck. "I hope you find something better than this."

"Come with me." Elizabeth didn't know why the words tumbled from her mouth other than she could see the sadness in her friend's eyes. Still, it was a ridiculous offer. She didn't have a ticket for Mary, but maybe she could exchange her ticket for two tickets somewhere closer. It might take her longer to get to her destination, but it would be worth it to see her friend get out as well.

Mary merely smiled sadly and shook her head. "I would love to, but I can't. There's nowhere for me to go and I'm too old to marry and start over."

"No, you're not. Look out west there are more men than women. I'm sure you could find a good man who would marry you and if not, you could stay with me."

"No, my place is here. I don't know anything other than

working for Jacob and Luther, but you go. Get out while you can."

Elizabeth wanted to argue with her, but there was no time. She wanted Mary to get out as well, but if the woman didn't want it for herself yet, there really was nothing Elizabeth could do. She pulled the woman close once more. "I'll pray for you, and if you do ever leave, maybe we can reunite one day."

"Maybe. Now you better get out of here. It's almost time for the evening shift to begin and Luther will be looking for you. I'll tell him you're sick to buy you some time."

That excuse wouldn't buy much time - Luther didn't believe an illness should keep you from working - but Elizabeth looked at her friend a moment longer, wishing there was something else she could say to get the woman to go with her. "Thank you," she said instead, knowing it was no use. She flashed a small wave and then hurried back down the stairs and out of the building. If she ever had a chance, she'd come back for Mary, she promised herself. The woman might not think she did, but Elizabeth knew she deserved a better opportunity.

As soon as she stepped outside, she glanced around. Though the sun shone warmly on her, there was a cold dread on her spine that someone was watching, that Luther knew what she was doing and would stop her before she could get on the train or that Jacob had seen her at the train station and would be waiting for her when she arrived again. She shook her head to clear the negative thoughts, and clutching her bag to her chest, she hurried as quickly as she could toward the train station, glancing every few seconds to the left and right to see if anyone was following her.

When she reached the station and stepped into the bustling crowd, she relaxed slightly, but only slightly. Twenty minutes still remained before the train left, and until she was seated and the train was pulling out of the station, she knew she wouldn't rest easy.

Hurrying to platform two, she joined the crowd boarding the train.

"Do you have a bag to check, Miss?"

"Excuse me?" She turned to see a man in a dark red uniform staring at her.

"A bag? Do you have a bag to check?"

She clutched her bag tighter to her chest. "No, only this one. Am I allowed to keep it with me?"

He smiled. "Of course, Miss. Let me help you aboard."

"Do you need to see my ticket?" She shifted the bag into one arm so she could reach for the paper that represented her freedom.

"No, Miss, the conductor will take that on the train."

"Oh, okay, thank you." She allowed him to help her step into the train car and then she hurried to find a seat. She chose one near the window so she could see not only the sights as they traveled, but so she could watch for any sign of Luther or Jacob before they left the station. Not that she had any idea what she would do if she did see them.

Her eyes scanned every person in the crowd, her heart beating loudly in her chest. How much longer until they departed? She glanced around for a clock, but there was none on the train. Finally, she heard a voice announcing the final boarding call and her heart began to relax. She was going to make it. She was going to get out.

"Is this seat taken?"

Elizabeth glanced up to see an elderly woman looking down at her. She shook her head and the woman sat down.

"Thank you. I feel like I've been on my feet all day. Where are you headed, my dear?"

"West." Though the woman seemed harmless, Elizabeth had no idea who she was or if she might be connected to Luther or Jacob.

The woman smiled as if she understood Elizabeth's hesitation. "I am too. I was attending my daughter's wedding in Chicago, but now I'm headed back to my home in Texas."

"That must be hard having her so far away." Elizabeth had no children yet, but she could imagine.

The woman nodded. "It is, but she always dreamed big and small-town life didn't suit her. Even though I miss her terribly, I'm glad she's happy. What about you? Are you married?"

"I..." Elizabeth paused as she considered how much to say. It was doubtful this woman knew Luther or Jacob, but Jacob seemed to have his hands in everything. What if he was connected to the daughter or the daughter's new husband? But this woman was going back home. Any word she could send to her daughter would take days if not weeks and why would she discuss a stranger on a train anyway. Surely, the woman was just being friendly. "I'm not currently, but I'm hoping to soon. I've had trouble finding a man who will handle my independence."

The woman chuckled. "I understand that. I have an independent streak too. Thankfully, I found a man who was willing to put up with me. I have no doubt that you will also."

"How long will it take us to get there?"

The older woman's brow lifted as if putting together that this was Elizabeth's first voyage that direction. "It's a two day trip from here to North Texas. Of course then you'll have to take a stagecoach to your final destination unless you're going to a town on the line."

Elizabeth wasn't sure exactly where Sage Creek was in Texas, but she rather doubted it was a town on the line. She pulled her ticket out and looked down at the destination city. Amarillo. She supposed she'd be asking around when she arrived there about how to get to Sage Creek. At least it would give her time to send word to Mr. Baxter about her arrival as well. Tucking her ticket back into her pocket, she looked back up at her companion and smiled.

"Thank you. Can you tell me about life out West? Do you work?"

The woman looked as if she was going to ask Elizabeth more about her destination but then decided against it. "Life out West isn't for everyone, but I enjoy it. My husband is a rancher, so I help him with that as well as taking care of the house, but I am also employed for myself."

Elizabeth's eyes widened. "You are? What do you do?" She'd heard of a few women opening stores in the east but only recently and she'd doubted any woman held a business in the much less developed west.

"I'm a seamstress. I don't own a shop or anything, but women bring their ideas to me and I make them dresses. It doesn't bring in much money, but it's something that's mine."

A tiny gasp flitted from Elizabeth's throat before she could stop it. "A seamstress? That's a dream of mine, but I didn't think it was possible as most women make their own clothes."

The woman nodded. "That is true, but there is a small change occurring. With women taking on more teaching positions and helping their husbands, they have less time to make their own clothing. In Chicago, it's happening even faster. I have orders from several of my daughter's friends."

"Wow, I had closed myself off to the possibility." For a moment, Elizabeth allowed her mind to wander to the idea of having her own store once again.

The woman placed a hand on her arm. "Never close yourself off to possibility. God has a plan for your life and sometimes it even matches your own."

Elizabeth nodded. She knew that God's plan was always best; she just wasn't sure if she was following God's plan or her own currently. In fact, she didn't know how any of this - losing her father, being forced to work for Jacob, running away - fit into God's plan, but she would trust that it did.

CHAPTER 7

Elizabeth

Elizabeth inhaled deeply as she poked her head out of the dusty coach. She'd never thought she would miss the smell of the outside, but after two days on the train and another day stuffed in the much smaller carriage, she couldn't get enough of the open air. Thankfully, the time had given her the ability to send word to Carl of her arrival, but she couldn't say she had enjoyed the journey. Not only had she been worried that Jacob would be waiting for her at every stop, but she hadn't slept well, not having the money for a sleeping car. Add in the odor of people and the need to sit most of the time, and to say she was glad to have arrived and be able to stretch her limbs would be an under-statement..

She looked around the town and marveled at how different it was from Chicago, more different than she would have imagined. Instead of a bustling town filled with many roads, the sounds of buggies and people, and colorful stores, this place was empty and brown. All of the buildings, not that there were many, were brown. Nearly the same shade of brown as the landscape so that they almost seemed to blend into each other.

The driver took her lone bag and helped her down, and as he handed the bag back to her, a large man approached her. He towered over her both in height and in girth and had a slight limp as he neared, but she did not shy away. Unlike the men she had just left, this one didn't seem as foreboding. Yes, he was formidable, but there was a gentle air about him. She prayed her instincts were correct for if they were not, this man could easily squeeze the life out of her body.

He took his hat off and his dark hair moved slightly in the breeze. "Miss Parker?" His voice was deep but soft at the same time, and as she looked closer, she could see the traces of nervousness in his darting eyes and the excessive swallowing in his throat. It wasn't like he was trying to lie to her, more like he was afraid to look her in the eye and hold the gaze. Why was he nervous?

"I am. I presume you are Mr. Baxter?" He was not exactly the way she had pictured him, but he had not lied about his traits.

He nodded and held out a hand. It was strong and calloused - definitely a hand that saw hard work. She blinked at it for a moment. Was it customary to shake hands with women here? As he didn't lower it, she placed her hand in his and let him pump her hand once.

"Do you need anything else in town or are you ready to proceed to the church?"

"Already?"

A light pink flashed across Carl's cheeks. "I took the liberty of informing Pastor Lewis of our marriage when I received word of your expected arrival. I assumed that you wouldn't feel comfortable under the same roof unless we were married. Was I mistaken?"

"No, not at all." Elizabeth should have been prepared for this, but she supposed in her mind that she had thought he would put her in a hotel and court her for a few days to make sure marriage was the right step. Or at least put her in a hotel for a night so that she could bathe and make herself presentable. There had been no way to freshen up on the coach and Elizabeth had no doubt that she looked a mess. While she knew this was not a marriage based on love, she could not deny the want to at least wash her face and comb her hair. "If there is a room at the church where I may change and freshen up that would be acceptable. If not, is there such a room nearby?"

Carl hooked his thumbs in his trousers and looked about. "I'm not certain if there is a room like that in town other than at the inn, but there is a small washroom at the church."

Elizabeth took a deep breath and nodded. "That will do then."

Carl gave a single nod in response, replaced his hat, and then held out his hand for her bag. She hesitated, wanting to hold on to it. After all, it held everything she owned in the world, but she worried he might take the gesture as a slight, and to be truthful, she was tired. Three long days with jittery nerves and little sleep was certainly taking its toll on her. Letting him carry the bag for a short time would be welcome. She allowed him to take the bag, and though she knew it was heavy, he hefted it as though it was no more than a sack of feathers. "Is this all you have?" he asked, his eyes darting around for the rest of her things.

"This is almost all I own. The bank took most of what my father still owned and what they didn't was placed in storage until I can show them proof of marriage." There were a few things she had left at the saloon that she wished she could have taken, but she wasn't going to mention that. He might send her back if he knew she'd been working at a saloon.

He considered her for a minute before nodding. "If you'll follow me then."

"Your limp. Is it serious?" she couldn't help asking as he led the way to an open wagon. It would change nothing, she'd given her word after all, but if it would require extra care, she felt it only fair to know up front.

He smiled at her as he placed her bag in the back. "Not too serious. I was a little careless this morning in my rush to come get you, and I wasn't paying attention to where my horse was stepping until he landed on my foot. It aches a little, but I'm sure it will be fine."

"Have you had a doctor check it?" she asked as she took his proffered hand and climbed into the wagon.

He chuckled. "No. Doc Moore has his hands full with other patients. He doesn't need to tell me my foot is bruised. If it gets worse, I'll go see him."

"But what if it's broken?" she asked. "Won't walking on it make it worse?"

"It's not broken, I promise," he said, as he limped over to the driver's side of the wagon. "If it was, I wouldn't be able to walk at all. We may only have one official doctor, but out here you learn a lot about medical care in the field, and I promise you this is nothing."

Deciding this was not an argument she was going to win, she simply nodded and looked around. "Is the church very far?"

He sat down beside her and took the reins. "It's just down there." He pointed to the far end of town. "Not far at all, but I figured you wouldn't want to walk all the way there on our dusty roads. Plus, my foot could use a rest."

While considerate, Elizabeth doubted she could get any dirtier from walking than she'd gotten just from riding in the dusty coach, but she said nothing and instead tried to familiarize herself with the town as they rode through it.

There was a general store though it looked much smaller than the one she was familiar with back in Chicago. A man with dirty blond hair leaned against the railing. His eyes were closed but his lips moved slightly making her wonder if he was talking to himself or simply dreaming. Then, a saloon came into view, quite similar to the one she had left, and she suppressed a shudder as she thought back to her time spent there. She hoped she would never have to do anything like that again. A small hotel was on the way as was an eatery. She wondered if her soon-to-be-husband ever ate there though she doubted it. Even in Chicago, restaurants were considered a luxury and not often attended.

Finally, they pulled up in front of a quaint clapboard church. The white siding appeared to have been freshly painted and though the place was not nearly as large as the church she left in Chicago, it was welcoming.

Carl tied up the horse and then helped her down before retrieving her bag. "Does this have everything you need?"

"Yes, thank you." Her possessions might be few, but her bag did contain her nicest dress and shoes, a brush, and a small mirror that she could use if the washroom was without.

She clutched the bag to her chest and followed Carl into the church. Like the outside, the inside boasted a welcoming atmosphere. Rows of pews filled each side of a middle aisle that led to the front. A small piano sat to one side and a simple pulpit stood in the middle. A man wearing all black except for the small white square designating him as a man of the cloth looked up from the pulpit as they entered.

"Welcome. You must be Miss Parker. I'm Pastor Lewis." A warmth emanated from the man as if he was personally blessed by God, and Elizabeth immediately felt comfortable in his presence.

"I am. Would you be able to point me to the washroom before we begin?"

The pastor smiled. "Of course. Follow me." He led her to a small doorway behind the pulpit and opened the door for her. "My quarters are to the left but you'll find the wash-room to the right."

"Thank you." Elizabeth followed his directions and found herself in a room much smaller than the ones she had become accustomed to at home. It was big enough for her to change but just barely. However, she was delighted to see a wash basin with a mirror above it. At least she wouldn't have to try and fix her hair using her much smaller mirror, and the water in the basin appeared clean. She wondered how often the pastor changed it or if he had done it specifically for this visit.

She washed her face first and brushed her hair, twisting it into the current style and securing it with pins. Then she pinched her cheeks to bring a little more color to them and pressed her lips together to do the same. Finally, she changed out of her soiled dress and into the nicest one she had in the bag. It was slightly wrinkled due to its time in the carpet bag, but that could not be helped and somehow she doubted that Mr. Baxter would care too much.

When she had also changed her shoes, she appraised her appearance once more in the mirror, decided it would do, and returned the soiled clothes to the carpet bag to be washed later. Then she took a deep breath and returned to the pulpit where the men stood waiting for her.

As the pastor began speaking, she took the time to look at the man who would now be her husband. She felt that he would be safer than Jacob, but that did nothing to quell the nerves bunching in her stomach. Would he be a good man? Would she adjust to this life so very different from the one she'd left? Would she be able to fulfill her wifely duties to him and would he give her time to adjust?

"Do you Carl Baxter take Miss Parker as your lawfully wedded wife, to honor and care for as long as you live?"

"I do," Carl said and the pastor turned to her.

"Do you Elizabeth Parker take Mr. Baxter as your lawfully wedded husband, to honor and care for as long as you live?"

"I do," Elizabeth said, her voice shaking only slightly. This was not how she'd imagined her life going, but as she looked at the man before her, she realized he was a decent looking man. Maybe not the kind that would have grabbed her fancy if they'd passed on the streets - he was larger than the picture of her perfect man and his face looked a little more weathered and hard than she would have wanted, but there was a kindness in his eyes and a gentleness in his touch as he held her hands.

"Then by the power given to me by the great state of Texas and the Lord Almighty, I pronounce you husband and wife."

"Thank you, Pastor," her husband said, clearly declaring the end to the ceremony.

The pastor nodded and wished them well before retiring to the back room.

"I guess you'd like to see the homestead now," Carl said.

Elizabeth wasn't sure about that. She imagined the homestead would be as simple as the town, and she doubted there would be much to see, but she kept those words to herself. "I cannot think of anything else I should be doing."

"All right then, let's go."

As he helped her back into the wagon, Elizabeth felt a tremor race down her spine. She glanced around, looking for any person that appeared out of context. She doubted that Jacob Canfield would follow her all the way out here, and she'd been careful about covering her tracks when she left, but that knowledge did nothing to dispel the fear that seemed to envelop her. Perhaps it was simply a fear of the unknown. She was about to embark on a journey she had never expected - in a new town, married to an unfamiliar man, and with no idea of what would be expected of her. Yes, that had to be it. Fear of the unknown and nothing more. She would continue to repeat those words over in her head until they rang true in her heart.

CHAPTER 8
Carl

As Carl neared his homestead, he tried to see it with fresh eyes. It was his home and he had worked hard to build it, so there was a sense of pride in his chest that could not be taken away, but Elizabeth was a proper woman from the city and he wondered how she would see it.

As the small cabin came into view, he felt her tense beside him. She said nothing, had said nothing since they left the church, only sat ramrod straight in the seat beside him, but he could feel it in her presence. The cabin was small, but it was large enough for him. There was a main room, a kitchen with a small table where he ate, and his bedroom. There was not much more, but he hadn't had need for much more.

"It's very quaint," Elizabeth said as he pulled the horse to a stop in front of the cabin. "How many rooms?"

"Just the one bedroom, but there's room to build when..." he trailed off as a red heat climbed his neck. He'd been about to say when children came into the picture, but he realized he had not discussed this with Elizabeth and he didn't want her to think he expected them right away. From the rosy pink coloring her cheeks, it was obvious she knew what he'd been about to say. "When it becomes necessary," he finished.

"Ah, yes, I see." She held her bag tightly in her delicate hands, so tightly that the knuckles of her hand were turning white. "Will we be sharing that room tonight then?" Her words came out scratchy and in a halting manner as if merely forcing them from her throat and across her lips caused her great discomfort.

"I can sleep on the couch in the main room until..." he again let the words die out, but this time because he wasn't sure how to finish them. He wanted her to be comfortable with him, but what if that never happened? Never sharing a bed with her wasn't an option as he wanted a family, but he also didn't want to give her a firm set of days in case it would fluster her too much and cause her to decide that she no longer wanted to engage in this agreement. They were officially married, but he did not know if there were clauses to mail-order bride contracts. Perhaps he should have learned more about them before now.

"Ah, yes. That will be agreeable then."

He tried not to feel slighted by the intense look of relief that crossed her features. "Let me get you set up in the bedroom."

She nodded and allowed him to help her down. Then she

waited, still clutching her bag like a barrier between them, while he led the way into the cabin.

The main room was sparse but furnished with a couch and a chair that he'd made himself. The table in the kitchen was also made by hand and would suffice until children came into the picture. He opened the door to his bedroom, a simple room with a bed, a dresser for clothes, and a table next to the bed that held his Bible at night and a candle he could light so he could read at night. "I hope this will be satisfactory."

"Do you have no mirror?" she asked, glancing around the room.

"Haven't felt the need for one, but we can pick one up in town if you'd like." He'd saved a few dollars in the time he'd waited for her to arrive for this very purpose. He hadn't known what she might like but wanted to have the means to provide what he could.

"I can do without for a time. I have a small one with me." She glanced around again. "I suppose you have no indoor washroom?"

The heat climbed his face once again. Jesse had mentioned this to him - that women preferred to have a washroom in the house and not outside - but he hadn't had the time or the means to build one yet. "I don't currently, but it is something we can look at adding on to the homestead."

The color drained from her face slightly but she nodded. "That would be lovely. You mentioned housework in your ad. Other than keeping the house in order and cooking, will you be expecting anything else of me?"

Carl had hoped she would have some knowledge of a farming life, but from the appearance of her hands, he wondered if she'd used them for any work at all. "Eventually, I would like to teach you the intricacies of farming so you can help in the field, but for now, perhaps you can feed the animals closer to the house, grab the eggs from the chickens and such?"

"I believe I can do that. Do you have a garden as well?"

He blinked in surprise at her question. "A small one, but there is space if you would like to grow more."

"Thank you. That would be very nice."

Silence fell between them then, and Carl realized he knew very little of this woman. He wondered if there would be many uncomfortable pauses like this between them or if they would become companions as Kate and Jesse had. He hoped for the latter and realized he might need to pick Jesse's brain to find out how to encourage the process.

"Well, I need to go check the fields. I will leave you to rest if necessary. Generally, I eat supper when the sun sets. Do you think you'll be able to work with that parameter or should I plan on fixing supper tonight?"

Elizabeth looked toward the small kitchen. "I am sure that I can find something to make."

Carl nodded, wishing he knew what else to say to her. This was more awkward than he'd expected. He clearly should have asked Jesse more questions. "That sounds fine. I'll be back at dusk."

It felt odd leaving a stranger in his house. It felt even more odd to know that stranger was now his wife. "Lord, please put your hand on this situation. Bless this marriage and help us to develop the kind of relationship that you would want us to have."

He glanced back at the homestead and wondered how long that might take.

CHAPTER 9
Elizabeth

E lizabeth wandered back into the bedroom and set her bag on the bed. His bed. Her husband's bed. The words felt odd and foreign in her mind even as she thought them. What had she been thinking leaving the only life she knew to come here to this foreign place with a man she didn't know? But she hadn't had a choice. Not really. She couldn't have stayed in Chicago and remained true to herself.

She sat on the bed, much harder and lumpier than the one she'd had back home, and wondered if she'd even be able to sleep here. There was nothing around. No pedestrians, no sounds from carts, no street lamps. It must get frightfully dark in the evenings and she wondered how Carl lit the cabin in the evening. Yes, there was a candle on the table, but it wouldn't give much light. He must have lamps somewhere. Perhaps she should go looking for them just in case.

She decided to unpack her clothes first, refolding the few dresses she'd brought with her to place in the dresser in the room. As she opened the drawer, she realized his clothes were already filling some of the room. What should she do about them? Did she leave them? Take them out? And if she did, where did she put them? Leaving them seemed to be the best option, so she did and simply put her things to the side. It wasn't like she had many anyway. Leaving as quickly as she had forced her to be choosy in what she took with her.

With her dresses unpacked, she took the quilt out and added it to the bed. Even if it didn't get cold enough to use it, just being able to see it made the room feel a bit more like home, but only a bit. It would definitely need more touches to feel like hers.

She scanned the small room one more time, looking for anything that might tell her more about Carl, but other than his clothes, there was nothing personal in the room. Perhaps the rest of the house would hold more clues. So, grabbing the dress she needed to wash, she wandered into the main room.

It was simple, with the only furniture being the couch, a chair, and a small table, but the furniture did look sturdy and hand made. Had he made it himself? There was no sewing basket by the chair like she'd had back home, but she could do without for now, and she was relieved to see a lantern on the table. The room also had a large fireplace, but still nothing that would tell her much about the man who lived here.

She wandered into the kitchen and took stock of what he had. Pots, plates, cutlery, but not a lot when it came to cooking. There was flour, corn, some canned foods, and what looked like vegetables though they were nearing the end of their edibility from the looks of it. She'd check the garden next to see if anything could be added, however, it appeared a stew would be in order tonight. It was the only way she could think to make the vegetables palatable. There was no meat lying about and none in the small ice box he had, so she made a mental note to look for a shed. He probably had meat in there.

On the small table, she found the first personal items she'd seen - a ceramic mug, which meant he was likely a coffee drinker like her father had been, and his Bible. Well, coffee she could certainly do, and the tension in her heart eased a bit with the realization that he probably read his Bible as much as she did. Perhaps they could read together as she and her father had done before he'd gotten sick. After she washed her dress and made dinner of course. If she could find everything she needed.

She decided to prepare the meal first and draped her soiled dress across the back of a chair. Then, grabbing the largest pot she could find, she began chopping up the vegetables and adding them. When that chore was finished, she grabbed her dress and wandered outside to survey the rest of the area and search for a wash tub.

She found a tin tub with a washboard near a water pump, so she filled the tub and washed her dress first and then hung it on the line to dry. Then she turned her attention to the garden. The little garden was lacking but well maintained. She hadn't been the biggest gardener back in Chicago, but she could probably figure out how to keep what he had planted growing and maybe she could find someone who could tell her if any crops that would grow well here were missing.

A few carrots and potatoes looked ready, so she pulled them up, but with no basket to put them in, she simply cradled them in her arms. Then she surveyed the rest of the area. There were two small buildings a few dozen feet from the house. The smaller one was no doubt the outhouse. She shuddered at the idea of having to traipse out there every time the urge hit, but she could do it. It was better than life with Jacob. The other building was a little larger and probably held the meat. She headed that direction to see if there was any meat she could add to the stew to help with the stock.

Even in the bright sunlight she shivered when she opened the door. Not only was the shed much darker inside, but the rows of deceased animals hanging from the ceiling were a little unnerving. Thankfully, near the back, she found some meat she thought might do. She untied it as quickly as she could and hurried out of the shed. Perhaps she could ask Carl to get the meat she would require daily so that she needn't venture in the shed often.

With that job done, she returned to the kitchen, cut up the meat and the few carrots and potatoes she'd brought in and added them to the pot. After rummaging a little more, she managed to find some herbs that she hoped would help and added them. Then she glanced out the window. The sun was lower in the sky, but not setting just yet. She wondered if she should start the stew now or give it a little longer. She decided to fire it up and just keep the flame low. She could always remove it from the heat and let it sit if he took longer than she expected.

With her womanly duties done, she wandered around the small house aimlessly. What in the world was she going to do to keep herself busy here? Yes, she had her sewing but with no new fabric, there would be little to sew on, and she didn't have the money to purchase much new fabric. She had her Bible, so there was plenty of reading she supposed, but even though she loved being in God's word, she didn't think she could fill all the time in the evening with that. Gardening and cleaning wouldn't take up her entire day, but maybe Carl would teach her what else she could do to help. Though she did not miss working in the saloon, she did miss the bustle of the city and the availability of stores. At least in Chicago, she could have walked the streets and looked in the windows to pass the time.

Well, there weren't shop windows here, but there were items that needed to be purchased. If she could find some paper and a pencil, she could write them down for the next time they went into town.

He had no writing desk like she'd had back home, but after a few minutes of searching, she was able to find some paper and a pencil. Sewing basket was the first thing she wrote down, along with supplies for sewing. She'd brought what she could with her, but she could use more string.

Plus, she should add some yarn for knitting. There had been some still attached to her mother's needles, but it wouldn't last long. A basket for collecting food was the next item added to the list along with some food items she would like to pick up. Of course she would ask him tonight if he perhaps had the items somewhere she hadn't looked, but if not, they would need to be picked up. Then she wrote down fabric. She would need some new dresses having left most of hers behind when she fled.

Dresses. The mere word gave her pause. Before her father got sick, she'd often spent hours sketching designs. It was a lofty goal, she knew that, but even if she could only sew for friends like the lady she'd met on the train, it would be worth it to her to see the joy on their faces. Could she do that here? She allowed her mind to imagine it for a few minutes and then shook her head. That would be silly. Not only would women here probably not be interested in her designs, but setting up something like that might draw attention to her name, and while she didn't think Jacob knew where she had gone, she couldn't be too careful. After all, Margaret had mailed the letter so she might remember the address, and she'd told Mary she was going west. She didn't think her friend would deliberately tell Jacob where she'd gone, but she had no doubt he could break her if he knew she had the information. No, a dress-making business would never be a realized dream now, and she would just have to get used to that.

Perhaps she couldn't start a business, but that didn't have to stop her from drawing. Without even realizing she was doing it, her hand began to sketch one design and then another. It was only when she realized the image was hard to see that she glanced up and realized the sun was setting. Oh no. He would be home soon and she hadn't checked the stew.

After lighting the lantern to give her more visibility, she checked the stew, relieved to see it had not burned. In fact, it looked perfect. The only question was if Carl would return in time to eat the stew while it was still warm?

She sat down at the table unsure if she should eat without him or not. It seemed rude to do so, but then again, her stomach had been making very unladylike noises recently and she had no idea when he would return. What if something happened to him out on the acreage? How would she even know? And if something did happen, what would she do? Carl had mentioned a Doc Moore, but she had no idea how to reach him. She didn't even know how to get back to town. With a sinking feeling, she realized she knew very little about her new life and for the first time, it scared her.

Thankfully, she didn't have to worry long as the front door opened and Carl entered.

"Sorry, I'm late. One of the cows was being stubborn tonight and my foot slowed me down."

Though she wasn't familiar with his normal look, he appeared more tired than he had earlier. His broad shoulders rounded forward slightly, and there was a haggard appearance to his face that she hadn't noticed when he left earlier.

"Oh, I'm sorry to hear that. Are you sure we shouldn't take you to see the doctor?"

Carl shook his head. "I'll check it again in the morning, but I'm sure it will be fine."

Elizabeth knew better than to continue arguing with him. Her father had been just as stubborn, but it didn't make her feel any better. "Well, I made stew for dinner and it's ready. Did you already wash up?"

Oh dear, was that even proper to ask? She always washed up before she ate, but perhaps he didn't. Could she live with a man who didn't practice proper hygiene?

His lips pulled into a slight smile as he looked at her. "I did and stew sounds amazing. I can't tell you how nice it is to come in after a hard day of work and realize the food is made. I've been living off canned beans and whatever I could cook quickly for too long."

"Well, I hope the food is to your liking," she said as she stood and moved to the stove to serve the stew.

"I have no doubt it will be. It smells wonderful in here."

It did? Elizabeth sniffed the air inconspicuously. She supposed there was a smell of vegetables permeating the air that was comforting, but she wished she'd had more spices to add. Picking up the ladle, she filled both bowls and carried them back to the table, setting one before her husband and then taking her own place.

"And it looks great too," he said softly. "Let's give thanks because I'm famished."

Elizabeth bowed her head and listened as Carl thanked

the Lord for health, home, and sustenance, and then she waited for him to take the first bite.

"Very good indeed." He barely looked up from the bowl as he shoveled another spoonful in.

"Thank you." Elizabeth smiled, glad that he seemed to be enjoying her food so much. "I hate to ask, but do you think we could return to town soon? There are some spices and food items I'd like to pick up as well as some fabric for more dresses."

His eyes lifted to hers but before he could say anything, she hurried on. "I have a little money to cover it if necessary."

He swallowed his bite of food and grinned at her. "That won't be necessary. I saved money in anticipation of you coming. We can go in tomorrow early. I have some things I need for the farm as well."

A feeling of relief flooded Elizabeth. She had felt he was different from Jacob, but now he was proving it. "Thank you."

"Of course." The rest of the dinner passed in silence, and though it was mildly uncomfortable, Elizabeth wasn't sure how to fill it.

After dinner, he retired to the living area and sat down with his Bible. "Will you join me?" he asked as she began placing the bowls in a tub to wash them.

She wanted to, but she didn't want to shirk her duties. "Oh, I need to take care of the dishes, but you go ahead."

He placed the Bible on the table and stood, coming to her side. With a gentle hand, he touched her arm, causing her to pause in her efforts. "The dishes can wait. I'll even fill the tub for you myself after. I would really like for you to join me."

"Very well." Elizabeth smiled as she followed him to the main room. She sat on the couch while he sat in his chair. It had been a while since she'd had someone read the Bible to her as her father had been too ill before he passed and after that, she'd been staying in the saloon so there was very little Bible reading there. She hadn't really thought this would be a part of her life again.

Carl cracked the Bible open and began reading. Elizabeth liked the sound of his voice. It was deep and melodious and reminded her of music she'd once heard wafting out from a dance hall. He was a good reader, giving inflection to the words and not halting or stumbling very often.

When he was finished, he asked her if she had any questions. She shook her head. The reading had been fairly straightforward and easy to understand.

"Perhaps another time then," Carl said, closing the book and placing it on the nearby table. "Let me get you that water." Effortlessly, he took the tub of dishes outside, returning a few minutes later. He placed the tub in the kitchen and returned to his chair. When his eyes closed, Elizabeth took that as her cue to finish her work in the kitchen.

Before she was done, she heard the sound of even breathing followed by an occasional snore. She wondered if she should wake him to have him move to the couch. It would surely be more comfortable or perhaps she should simply place a blanket over him and leave him to figure it out. Uncertain, she chose the latter option as it seemed less invasive, and with that task done, she continued to the bedroom and shut the door.

She stepped out of her dress, folding it neatly to sit atop the dresser before climbing into the bed. It was a strange sensation, sleeping in someone else's bed. Not only was the mattress unfamiliar, but she couldn't help picturing Carl sleeping under these covers just the night before and that led her mind to wander to when he might ask for his bed back. They were married, and he had every right to share the bed as her husband, but the thought still gave her trepidation.

She'd had little physical interaction with men, having been too independent when she was younger and then too busy once her father got sick, and the thought of any sort of intimate touch gave her pause. It would be a hurdle she would have to address soon, but for tonight, she would push it from her mind and enjoy the feeling of relief of being away from the saloon. And Jacob.

CHAPTER 10
Carl

Carl woke the next morning to the sounds of breakfast being made in the kitchen. His eyes snapped open to realize there was also light in the cabin. He was usually up before the sun, so how had he slept so long? But as he moved to get up, he realized how. There was a massive crick in his neck from sleeping in the chair. No doubt he hadn't slept well from the position he'd been in. He stretched and massaged his neck, and when he felt like the pain had lessened, he stood. At least his foot seemed better this morning. There was less pain as he made his way into the kitchen.

"Good morning," Elizabeth said, putting a plate of breakfast on the table. "I wasn't sure if I should wake you or let you sleep."

"I'm usually up before the sun, so you won't have to worry about it, but I suppose I'm glad we decided to go to town today so I don't feel so behind on my chores." He pulled out his chair and sat down, his stomach rumbling at the delicious aroma of the plate before him.

"Thank you again for taking me today. I know it takes time away from your work, but maybe I can help when we return."

"Perhaps." He did hope that Elizabeth would be able to help soon, but he didn't want to overwhelm her. It was only her second day here, and he had no doubt she was dealing with quite the adjustment.

After breakfast, he hitched the wagon and soon they were on their way into town. The ride was quiet but not entirely uncomfortable. Still, he was relieved when the general store came into view. He pulled the horses to a stop and jumped down to tie them before helping Elizabeth down.

He looked up at her as he held out his hand. She smiled as she placed her hand in his, but she let go as soon as her feet touched the ground. Carl tried not to see it as an affront. After all, they were still strangers, but he couldn't help wondering when that would change. When would she be comfortable around him? And perhaps more importantly, when would he be allowed back in his bed? He certainly couldn't afford any more late mornings.

The tiny bell jingled as they entered the store, and Mr. Brown looked up from the counter. He'd had the bell installed a year ago, even though the store wasn't big enough to need one. He'd claimed it was so he could hear people enter even if he was in the back, but as he was rarely anywhere other than behind the counter, Carl figured he had done it for the audible reminder of clients.

"Good morning, Carl. Who is this lovely lady with you?"

Carl glanced over at Elizabeth whose cheeks had turned a rosy pink color. "Good morning, Mr. Brown. This is my wife, Elizabeth. She arrived from Chicago yesterday and realized there were a few things she needed for the homestead." He stepped closer to Elizabeth and pointed to the far left corner of the store. "The fabric is in the back corner if you'd like to start there."

"That would be nice. Thank you."

As she walked away, he stepped closer to Mr. Brown, sure that the man would have questions.

"Chicago, huh? The mail-order bride ad?"

Carl nodded. "Thank you for helping me place that by the way. She's having to adjust to the smaller town, but I'm hoping I can introduce her to some of the women and make her feel more connected."

Mr. Brown nodded and scratched his chin as he watched Elizabeth. "Well, Mrs. Cook is usually in before noon to grab items for the clinic and the like. Maybe she can help."

"That's what I'm hoping. Thank you." Carl walked over to Elizabeth and watched as her fingers trailed over the fabric. It was clear that she had an eye for such things, and he wondered how much the particular piece she was looking at would cost him. He knew there would be more money involved once he married - after all, he was feeding another mouth as well - but he had forgotten that she might want to spend money on things he'd had no need of before - fabrics, perfumes, and the like. Where would that extra money come from? She'd said she'd brought a little with her, but could he really ask her to pay? After all, she'd left her entire life in Chicago to come and marry him. Yes, she'd done it willingly, but as a husband, wasn't it his duty to supply her needs as well?

"Do you like that one?" he asked as he stepped to her side.

Startled, she pulled her hand back before turning to look at him. "I do, but I don't have enough to afford it."

"How much is it?"

Her eyes widened and she shook her head. "No, I can't ask you to do that. It's too much."

"Why don't you let me be the judge of that? How much?"

"It's a dollar thirty for the bolt as it's silk." She pressed her lips together as his eyes grew. "It's too much and not necessary. It would be the perfect fabric for a lovely fancy dress, but I don't even know when I would need one now. It makes much more sense to get the more practical fabric." She reached for the print gingham that was a few bolts over and held it up. "This could make a lovely new dress and it's much more affordable."

"You seem to know quite a bit about fabric."

Elizabeth sighed. "Well, it is rather expected that women learn about fabric and sewing, but I've always enjoyed sewing. Back in Chicago, I used to dream about having my own dress shop where I could make clothes for other women."

Carl's brow lifted. "Why didn't you do it?"

Elizabeth smiled sadly and shook her head. "It's an unrealistic dream. Not only would it cost too much to open a store like that, but most women sew their own clothes. What need would they have of a seamstress? Plus, when my father got sick, all my time had to go into caring for him, and when he passed, there was no money."

"I'm sorry about your father, but I'm sure there are some women who do not find sewing as enjoyable as you do that would benefit greatly."

"That is true, but it wouldn't be affordable. You balked at the cost of simply purchasing the silk fabric. Imagine how much more expensive it would be if you had to pay someone to make the dress."

Carl's face paled for a second in shock before he shook his head. Knowing how tight money was in the town, he was almost certain no one would be able to afford that, but he didn't want to discourage Elizabeth either. "Perhaps they couldn't afford a fancy dress but could afford a print one."

Elizabeth pressed her lips together and looked back at the fabric. "I'm not sure. Obviously you know this town better than I do, but I can't imagine there are many women who could afford to purchase a dress rather than make it themselves."

"What about teaching them? Maybe they couldn't afford to buy a dress, but I know the women get together to quilt. What if you charged a small fee for lessons to help them improve?"

"It's possible, I suppose. Maybe when I know more people, I'll look into it."

Carl nodded. He could tell she was humoring him, but he wanted to get her involved in the town. He wanted her to be more comfortable, but he knew he couldn't push her too hard or she might shut down entirely. He just wished there was something he could do to help her feel more comfortable. Thankfully, the bell jingled again and Carl looked up to see Emma Cook enter. Things were still a little uncomfortable between them, but he knew that Emma would try to make the new woman feel welcome. "Mrs. Cook." He raised his voice to call his old friend over.

Emma looked up and offered a small smile. They had once been close, having grown up in town together, but Carl had strained the relationship by trying to get her to marry him when she wasn't interested. He'd apologized, but it was clear there was still some unease between them.

"Mr. Baxter," she said, using his proper name as well.

"I'd like to introduce my wife Elizabeth to you."

A flicker of surprise crossed Emma's features before she schooled her face and smiled widely at Elizabeth. "Elizabeth, what a pleasure to meet you." Emma extended her hand. "I'm Emma Cook. When did you get to town?"

"Just yesterday," Elizabeth said softly.

"Well, then you have to come to the sewing circle this Sunday. It will be a perfect place for you to meet some of the women of the town." She turned to Carl. "You'll bring her, won't you? William and I can take her home after so you don't have to make another trip."

"Of course." Carl nodded and offered her a relieved smile. This was exactly what he'd been hoping for.

"Wonderful. I can't wait to hear all about your journey and how you're liking the town," Emma said. "Don't forget to bring something to work on. I wish I could talk more now, but I'm in a bit of a hurry."

Carl turned to Elizabeth, expecting to see the same smile on her face that filled his, but instead an angry red colored her face and her eyes flashed at him. "Why didn't you ask if I wanted to go before accepting?" Elizabeth whispered.

Carl blinked at her, startled by her reaction. "I'm sorry. I didn't think it would be a big deal. I thought you would want to meet other women. Was I wrong?"

Elizabeth sighed and shook her head. "No, I'm sorry. I'm happy to meet other women, but I would appreciate it if you would ask me and not blindly accept things for me."

There was obviously something more behind her reaction, but Carl didn't want to press her for the information here. Still, he would have to probe more into the situation later. She had to understand that she couldn't address him that way in public. "I guess there are aspects to this marriage that we both need to adjust to."

She pressed her lips together and folded her arms across her chest. "I suppose there are."

Silence filled the space between them, and for a brief moment, Carl wondered if he'd made a terrible mistake. What if this woman was a shrew and wanted to rule the house that way? That was not the kind of woman he wanted to start a family with, but then he remembered that her life had recently been turned upside down. She'd lost her father and her home, and she was bound to need some time to adjust to this new life. He took a deep breath before speaking again. "Shall we get the rest of the items we need and be going then? I do need to get to work on the farm."

Elizabeth nodded, and they gathered up the rest of the supplies on her list before taking everything to the counter.

"It's so nice to meet you, Mrs. Baxter," Mr. Brown said as he began totaling their items. "I heard Mrs. Cook invite you to the sewing circle. That's a fantastic way to meet some of the women of the town."

"Yes, it sounds wonderful," Elizabeth said, but Carl could still hear the tightness in her voice. He'd only been trying to help, but he was beginning to wonder if they would ever have the kind of marriage that Jesse and Kate or William and Emma did.

CHAPTER 11
Elizabeth

Elizabeth could not calm the nerves rumbling around in her stomach. It was Sunday morning, and not only was it her first time attending church with Carl, which was nerve wracking in itself, but she was to meet with the women of the town afterwards for a sewing circle. She loved to sew, but she didn't have close female friends. Growing up, she'd always been too different, too independent. Even the girls she had been friends with when she was younger had lost touch with her once they were married. Other than Mary, the one woman at the saloon that she'd become close to before she left, Elizabeth had never really had female friends, but perhaps that was going to change today. Taking a deep breath, she pulled the bedroom door open and headed for the kitchen.

Carl turned at the sound of her footsteps and paused, the coffee urn in hand. "You look very pretty. Is that a new dress?"

Elizabeth glanced down at the dress. It wasn't new, but she'd stitched on some lace and a fancy pocket that seemed to give new life to the old garment. "No, but thank you." A soft heat crawled up her neck as she moved to start breakfast. Carl still hadn't poured the coffee or moved.

"Is your hair different too?"

Elizabeth's hand touched the back of her hair, pulled up in a twist on her neck. "Yes, I thought I should put it up for church. Does it look all right? I can change it down if not." It had been so long since she'd been in a church that she didn't really know what the right dress was, but she figured a proper hairstyle was expected.

"No, it looks fine. I just haven't seen it that way before."

"Oh, well, yes. It takes longer to put it like this, so I generally don't bother, especially if I'm going to be working around the house or in the garden as it will just fall out of place."

"That is understandable." But still he didn't move. Elizabeth wasn't sure what to make of his reaction. He was staring at her in a way that she wasn't used to, and it sent a small shiver down her spine. "Is everything all right?"

"What? Oh, yes, sorry." He turned to fill a cup with coffee, but Elizabeth did not miss the pink that blossomed up his neck. What did that mean?

Deciding she didn't have time to worry about it, Elizabeth dismissed the thought from her mind and began preparing breakfast. By the time it was ready, Carl was at the table with his Bible open and his coffee half gone.

"Would you like a refill?" she asked as she set a plate of Johnnycakes in front of him.

"Thank you. That would be nice."

Elizabeth nodded and took his mug to refill it.

"Did you attend church back in Chicago?" he asked as she lifted the kettle from the stove.

"I did, until my father got sick. Then it was hard to get him to go, and after he passed..." She paused, not wanting to tell him about her life after.

"I'm sorry," he said. "I didn't mean to bring up painful memories."

Elizabeth took her chair and poured syrup on her Johnnycakes. "No, that's okay. I miss my father, but I've missed attending church as well. I'm looking forward to attending with you."

"As am I. Shall we pray?"

As Carl prayed, Elizabeth found her eyes lifting to study him. Though he had a rough exterior, she had only seen the softer side of him. He was patient and kind with her, and though she doubted he enjoyed it, he had made no mention of reclaiming his bed yet. She had never cared for a man besides her father and she had no idea what love might feel like, but she could not deny that Carl made her feel safe.

The rest of breakfast passed in silence, but it was a comfortable one. Carl continued reading his Bible as he ate, and Elizabeth thought through scenarios of the day. She had no idea what to expect and her mind ran rampant with possibilities.

When breakfast was finished, Elizabeth grabbed the new

fabric they'd purchased and her sewing supplies and followed Carl outside. She waited on the porch while he brought the wagon around and when she had climbed into the wagon, Carl urged the horses towards town. It wasn't a long trip, but by the time they reached the outskirts of town, Elizabeth's stomach felt as if every fiber inside was bunched and knotted together.

"What do I do with my things?" Elizabeth asked as Carl tied the horses up.

"Leave them in the wagon. No one will mess with them." He held out his hand and helped her down, and for the first time, Elizabeth wanted to hold his hand a little longer. There was a silent strength that flowed from him that she wished she could siphon into her own resolve. She nodded and allowed him to lead her to the church.

The church looked even smaller when it was filled with people, but it was well-maintained and clean. Carl led her to a row and she slipped in, but she hadn't even taken a seat when people began coming up to them.

"Good morning, Carl," a man said. He was tall with dark hair and a dark-haired woman holding a baby was by his side. "I had heard that your wife arrived."

"Good morning, Jesse. Mrs. Jennings," Carl said as he shook hands with the man. "This is Elizabeth."

The man nodded. "Pleased to meet you, Mrs. Baxter. This is my wife, Kate."

The dark-haired woman smiled. "I'm so happy to make your acquaintance. Emma told me she invited you to the sewing social after church and I'm delighted that you'll be able to join us. I was new to this town myself, so I understand feeling a bit on the outside, but I think you'll find the women very welcoming here."

"Thank you. I'm looking forward to it." Elizabeth wasn't sure that was exactly the truth, but the nerves in her stomach had appeared to settle slightly so perhaps that was a sign.

As Jesse and Kate made their way to their seats, a few other people approached them. Carl introduced her to each one, but she doubted she would remember all the names, and she was beginning to wish people would just let her take her seat.

Finally, there was a tapping from the front, and she looked up to see Pastor Lewis smiling out at them. Just like the first time she'd met him, his smile exuded a warmth and calmed the nerves bunching in her stomach. "Good morning, everyone. It is such a blessed day and I know you are enjoying socializing with each other, but let's quiet down and turn our focus to the service."

He began with a few hymns that Elizabeth didn't know the words to. Carl sang beside her, but his voice was soft as if he either wasn't sure of the words or wasn't confident in his voice. It sounded pleasant to her, but she was no expert. When the songs finished, the sermon began. Pastor Lewis had a melodic voice and he was engaging, but Elizabeth still found it hard to concentrate on the words being said. Her mind remained focused on the sewing social afterwards.

Too soon, the sermon came to an end and the church

sang another song to end the service. Then Carl was leading her from the aisle.

"I'll take you to the barn where the women are meeting. Are you sure you're comfortable with Emma returning you? If not, I can stay." He said the words, but she could tell he didn't want her to ask him to stay. She knew he had work to do back at the farm, but she was touched that he even offered.

"I will be fine. It's just a group of women sewing. How bad could it be?" She didn't expect anything unusual to happen, but she'd been around enough women to know that wasn't always the case.

They exited the church and she followed him back to the wagon to grab her things and then to a small barn-like building about fifty feet away.

"This is our town hall and meeting place," he said. "At least for smaller groups or on Sundays when the church is in use. Otherwise, we generally just use the church."

"That makes sense," Elizabeth said. It wasn't like there were many other options in this small town for town meetings.

Before Carl even reached the door, it swung open and a startled Emma stared back at them. "Oh, sorry. I hope I didn't scare you. I was just going to see if Kate needed any help with the baby, but come on in, Elizabeth. I'm so glad you could join us, and I'll introduce you to the others before I go."

Though still nervous, Elizabeth nodded and followed Emma inside. Carl bid her farewell and then he was gone.

The area was a single room with no furniture besides the chairs arranged in a circle. There were five chairs but only two of them were taken at the moment.

"Elizabeth, I'd like you to meet my sister Carrie and our friend Sarah," Emma said, pointing to each girl as she said their name. Carrie looked a little younger than Elizabeth assumed Emma and Sarah were, but she had a kind face.

Sarah spoke first. "Nice to meet you, Elizabeth. You married Carl, is that right?"

Elizabeth nodded. "I did. I know it's not conventional, but when my father died, it seemed like a good opportunity."

"We know all about unconventional," Sarah said. "Have you met Kate yet?"

"I believe so. The woman with the baby, right?"

"Yep, that's her. She was a mail-order bride too though she wasn't supposed to marry Deputy Jennings."

"Her husband is a deputy?" Elizabeth hadn't seen anything on the man to denote him as law enforcement. Perhaps there was no need in a town this small.

"Not anymore. He stepped down when he found out Kate was pregnant, but he was."

"I see." Well, that explained the lack of a badge on him. "But what did you mean that Kate wasn't supposed to marry him?"

"While Sarah regales you with that story, I'm going to go check on Kate," Emma said, touching her elbow. "Will you be alright?"

"I think so. Thank you."

Emma slipped out the door and Sarah pulled Elizabeth to the empty seat between her and Carrie. "So, Kate had accepted a mail-order bride ad, but on her way here, her stage coach was robbed."

Elizabeth gasped and covered her mouth with her hand. She had never even considered getting robbed on her way here. Though her journey had been long, she was thankful it hadn't been dangerous. "That's awful. What did she do?"

"Well, the men wore masks, but she saw a scar on one of the men's hands. When she got to town, her betrothed picked her up, but she felt like something was off. Just before the ceremony, he took off his gloves and she saw the same scar. She was about to marry the man who robbed her."

The story sounded so unbelievable that Elizabeth wondered if Sarah was pulling her leg. However, the woman seemed earnest and Carrie was nodding along. "How did she get away?"

"She ran and stole a horse, but of course the guy chased her. By the time she reached Deputy Jennings, she was in bad shape and he had to help her. Kate had no money, having been robbed, so Deputy Jennings offered to marry her. Then it turned out that the man who had robbed Kate was also responsible for the death of Pauline, the woman Deputy Jennings was going to marry."

"Wait, he was engaged to another woman?"

"Before he became a deputy," Carrie said, trying to clarify the story. "It was after Pauline's death that he donned the badge to try and bring her killers to justice."

"Wow, that must have been hard for Kate to deal with."
She supposed she was glad that Carl didn't seem to come
with the baggage. At least, he hadn't mentioned being
married before and the homestead certainly didn't have a
woman's touch to it, but perhaps she should ask just to be
sure.

"It was tricky at first," Sarah continued, "but marrying
someone was the only way she could stay, so she accepted
his proposal, and their marriage eventually turned into one
of love. They make a wonderful pair though not everyone
was thrilled at first."

Elizabeth's brow wrinkled in confusion. "What do you
mean not everyone was thrilled at first?"

Carrie jumped in again, shooting a look at Sarah as if
silently telling her to stop talking. "Well, Pauline's family
still lives here. They thought Jesse was trying to replace her,
and Pauline's best friend, Rebecca, wasn't exactly thrilled
with Kate taking her place. It took them a while to accept
Kate, but things are better now."

"So, are you not friends with this Rebecca?" Elizabeth
had never had a close group of friends, so she wasn't sure
exactly how they worked, but in a town this small, she'd
assumed the women would all stick together.

"No, we are; she was invited but couldn't come today,"
Sarah said. "I'm sure you'll meet her soon though."

"I look forward to it," Elizabeth said as the door opened
and Emma re-entered followed by Kate who held a baby in
her arms. "What did we miss?"

"Nothing," Sarah said. "We were just filling Elizabeth in on how Kate came to our town."

Kate smiled. "Definitely not the way I planned it, but I'm glad it worked out. Where are you from, Elizabeth?"

"Chicago. I lived there my whole life, but it was just my father and me the last several years, and he passed away a month ago."

"I'm so sorry to hear that. Did you not have any other family in Chicago?" Kate set a bag down at one of the empty chairs before shuffling the baby to her other shoulder and sitting herself.

"Unfortunately not. My mother died in childbirth with my younger sister, and my father, though he thought he was doing the right thing, left a horrible man to look after me. I couldn't stay, so I decided the best way to get away from him was to leave Chicago and a mail order bride situation seemed like the perfect solution. It is more awkward than I thought it would be though."

Kate chuckled. "I know that feeling. It took some time for Jesse and me to bond, but keep praying about it and I have a feeling that God will bless your union."

Elizabeth smiled at the other woman. "I have been, but I'm still a little scared. I've never shared a bed with a man."

"Ah." Kate and Emma shared a look while Sarah and Carrie both looked away. "Yes, that is definitely an adjustment and was the biggest one for me as well, but I believe if you keep praying about it, God will give you peace." Kate looked over at Emma again as if urging her to jump in.

"I agree," Emma said, not quite meeting Elizabeth's eyes, "and Carl is a good man."

There was an awkward silence as the girls all exchanged glances. "Yes, he does seem to be," Elizabeth said, wondering what she was missing.

"Well," Emma said, breaking the awkwardness, "Shall we get to sewing then?"

"That would be lovely," Elizabeth said, relief coursing through her.

Emma pulled out the dress she was working on, and the rest of the women did the same. Elizabeth looked at what each woman was working on before she pulled out her fabric and began putting a rough pattern together.

"You're doing a whole dress?" Sarah asked.

"Um, yes. Do you not sew entire dresses?"

"Not without a clear pattern and even then, they never look as nice as I'd like them to."

"I'd be happy to show you how," Elizabeth said. "I've always had a passion for sewing. One day, I'd love to open a dress shop."

"That would be amazing," Sarah said. "I can't say that I love sewing, but then I don't love cooking either." She and Kate exchanged glances and then giggled as if sharing some private joke.

Elizabeth dropped her eyes to her lap, feeling very much like an outsider at the moment.

"Oh, I'm sorry," Sarah said, touching her arm. "I forgot that you don't know my history. My parents run the cafe in town, but I hate cooking. I'm a much better baker. When I first met Kate, she shared that she didn't like sewing even though her mother had sewn a lot. We thought it was funny that we didn't like what we seemed to grow up around."

"And that's why we have each other," Emma said. "We can share our gifts and talents with the others to help everyone."

As Elizabeth imparted her knowledge to the other women in the room, she began to feel like maybe she had found the place she was meant to be at last.

CHAPTER 12

Carl

Carl looked up from the fence he was repairing at the sound of the approaching wagon. It had to be Elizabeth returning, and he was eager to hear how her time had gone. He hoped it had gone well. Though their marriage was still only one of convenience, he liked Elizabeth and he wanted her to be happy. He didn't think she'd leave him if she wasn't content as she had no family to return to, but he'd heard of it happening before - women coming out west to marry only to realize it wasn't for them and leaving their husbands high and dry. No, he wouldn't let that happen. Even if this outing hadn't gone as he'd hoped, he would find a way to make Elizabeth happy.

After setting down his tools and wiping the sweat from his brow, he approached the wagon and held out his hand to help her down. "Thank you for bringing her home, William, Mrs. Cook." Though he no longer held any animosity towards William Cook, it was still awkward calling his childhood friend by her married name.

"It was our pleasure," Emma said with a smile as Elizabeth took his hand and climbed down. "Your wife is quite the seamstress and a lovely addition to our sewing circle."

Elizabeth chuffed away the compliment. "It was nothing. I just showed them a few tricks."

"A few tricks?" Emma chuckled and shook her head. "We were in awe, and we're trying to convince Elizabeth to open a shop where she can sell her designs and maybe teach sewing lessons. I think the town is ready for something like that."

"I told her the same thing," he said, reaching up for the bag Emma handed down. He was no expert on what the women of the town wanted or needed, but he was pleased to hear Emma agreed.

"Please think about it, Elizabeth. We'll see you next Sunday." She waved a farewell as William urged the horses forward.

"Well, it appears you made quite an impression," Carl said when the wagon was out of sight.

"She is kind, but I'm afraid I don't think she's right. Even in Chicago, these types of shops were just starting to open and few women could afford to frequent them." Elizabeth took her bag from him and began to walk toward the homestead.

Though he had work to finish, Carl hurried after her. "But that doesn't mean it couldn't work. There's always things to trade if people don't have money initially."

Elizabeth sighed as she opened the door. "I would love it, but I just don't see it happening. Everything is much simpler here and I doubt the women have the need for the kind of dresses I make."

"That might be true, but Emma was right that the town is growing and you never know when there will be a need. Besides, you sew things other than dresses, right?" Carl had seen her working on things in the evening, but he honestly had no idea whether they had been a dress or something else.

"I've been mainly working on repairing my old dresses, but I can sew other things - quilts and the like, but I still don't know if there's a market for those things here."

"Plus she mentioned lessons…"

"Perhaps back in Chicago that would have worked but here…" Elizabeth shook her head as she let the words fade out.

"I'll admit that I don't know much about sewing or about what women want or need from towns, but I've known Emma for years and I trust her. She grew up here and knows the people. If she says there's a desire for some-thing like that, then I think you should consider it. I'll even go into town with you to look for a place if you'd like or perhaps you could do it here."

Elizabeth set down her bag and then turned to him, her head cocked slightly to the side. "Why is this so important to you?"

Carl hesitated only a moment before stepping closer to her. "Because you're important to me. You're my wife now and I want you to be happy. If this makes you happy, then I think you should do it."

She held his gaze for so long that Carl wondered if he should make the move to touch her. He'd been thinking about it for the last few days, but he didn't want to rush her. Just as he gathered his nerve though, she shook her head. "No, it's a silly dream and I'd rather just let it go. If you don't mind, I think I'm going to retire to the room for a bit."

Carl nodded though he wanted to continue the conversation with her. He wanted her to open up and let him in, but he supposed that was going to take more time. As soon as the door closed, he sighed and grabbed his Bible. She might need time, but he was going to need God to help him through this.

CHAPTER 13
Elizabeth

E lizabeth closed the door and leaned against it for a moment, taking a few deep breaths to try and calm her racing heart. Carl had been looking at her as if he wanted to kiss her, and she wasn't sure she would have minded if he had. However, she wasn't ready for that, was she? It had been less than two weeks, and she knew that the day she let him kiss her, she had better be prepared for the rest of her wifely duties, so she'd kept her distance. But every day, she felt herself becoming more attracted to Carl. She liked how he read to her from the Bible after dinner. She enjoyed watching him enjoy her food, and now he was willing to help her open a dress shop? To fulfill her dream? What kind of man did that? But she knew that answer.

It was not only in his words just now, but in every one of his actions over the past several days. He wanted to provide for her, but he also wanted her to be happy and he was willing to lose her help at the farm to make that happen.

How had she gotten so lucky? Not only had she escaped Jacob, but she'd married a man better than she could have ever asked for.

Jacob. As his name registered in her head, her smile faded. It didn't matter how much Carl supported her, she couldn't open a store because she couldn't chance Jacob finding out about it. She doubted Sage Creek would care much, but what if a journalist came through and wrote about the store? Word might travel back to Chicago and reach Jacob. Of course, that assumed that a journalist would find the store an interesting story and write about it. It further assumed that said journalist would write a big enough piece for word to travel East. It then hinged upon whether Jacob would read or hear about the story. And finally, it relied on Jacob being able to determine that it was her store. She didn't even know if he knew that she liked to sew, and when she looked at all the steps that would have to be met, it did seem farfetched that opening a store would lead to her demise. So could she do it? Could she take a chance?

She wanted to open a shop with all her heart, and now she had not only the encouragement of a friend - was it too early to call Emma that? - but the blessing from her husband, so why was she hesitating? Was she so afraid of failure that she was terrified to even start? Was she so fearful of a farfetched scenario that she would let her dreams die? Was she so reluctant to have a real marriage with Carl that she would give up her desires to remain not alone but lonely for the rest of her life? No, she wasn't. Her father had taught her better than that.

Taking a deep breath, Elizabeth pulled open the door and walked back into the living room. Carl's face registered his surprise, but he said nothing as he waited for her to speak.

"I wasn't completely honest with you a minute ago. I would love to open a store, but I'm afraid. I'm afraid it will fail and I'm afraid that the man I ran from in Chicago will find me if I do."

Carl crossed the room and took her hand. For a second, Elizabeth worried he would pull her into an embrace, but as if sensing her unease, he merely led her to the couch. "What man?"

Elizabeth took a deep breath. "When my father died, he left a man to look after me. Jacob Canfield. Unfortunately, he was not the good man my father thought he was. He forced me to work in his saloon though only as a waitress," she said, dropping her eyes. "Still, I knew I couldn't stay, so I ran away. I'm sorry I didn't tell you earlier, but I was afraid that you wouldn't want to marry me if you knew."

Carl placed a hand under her chin and lifted her face to his. "I'm sorry you had to go through all of that, but I'm glad it led you here. To me. We are not defined by choices in our life made for us by others. We are not even defined by choices we make ourselves. We always have the opportunity to change and grow, and with God's help, we can become the people He planned us to be. I don't know if opening this store is God's will for you, but it seems like it's been a desire on your heart for a while, so we can pray about it, and if it is God's will, He will not only provide a place for you but will protect you if this man ever does happen to find you."

Elizabeth felt her protective shell begin to splinter. For so long, she had built up walls to keep others out so that she wouldn't have to feel the pain of losing someone again, but she hadn't realized until just this moment how utterly lonely she was. After the death of her mother, her father had been enough, but now with him gone, she needed someone. Someone to talk to, to hug her, to tell her everything would be all right even if it wasn't.

Elizabeth placed her hands on Carl's, removing them from her face so she could hold them in her lap. "Thank you for being so understanding. I had no idea what to expect when I came out here, but you have been more than I could ask for."

She felt like she should say more, but no more words would come, so she simply stared at him, and he returned her gaze. Then, slowly, he moved closer until his lips were mere millimeters from hers. He was waiting for her to pull back, to tell him this wasn't okay, but she wasn't going to do that. She still wasn't sure she was ready for everything else, but she was definitely ready for this, so she squeezed his hands to let him know and he closed the distance. His touch was soft and not demanding, but Elizabeth's heart began to hammer in her chest all the same. She had never been kissed by a man and hadn't known what to expect, but even her wildest imagination could not have created this - the flood of emotions coursing through her body.

Before she was ready for it to end, Carl pulled back and smiled at her. "I've got to finish my work tonight, but I can make some time tomorrow. How about we go into town and see what's available?"

"I'd like that."

Carl squeezed her hands again and then stood, giving her a final glance before exiting the homestead. For a moment, Elizabeth simply sat there, trying to process her emotions, but then she stood and decided to make the best dinner Carl had ever had.

The rest of the evening passed by as usual, but it felt different after the kiss they'd shared, and though Carl did not ask about joining her in the bedroom tonight, Elizabeth thought about it for the first time since she'd arrived.

CHAPTER 14

Carl

Carl smiled over at Elizabeth as they neared the town. Excitement radiated off her like rays of sunshine and had since she'd woken up this morning. She had carefully folded all her dresses into a bag to take with them just in case. He just hoped there would be a place to rent because he would hate to crush her spirits.

When they entered the town, he led the wagon up and down the main road first, searching for any empty buildings or signs, but there were none. That left only two options - the bank or Mr. Brown.

Because Mr. Brown owned the general store, he had his finger on everything that happened in town. If there was a space available, he would know about it, so Carl pulled the wagon up in front of the general store and jumped down.

"What are we doing here?" Elizabeth asked. "Did you need more items from the store?"

He smiled as he held out his hand. "No, but Mr. Brown

is a great resource in this town. He'll be able to tell us if there's any space for rent."

"Oh, okay." Though she didn't sound entirely convinced, Elizabeth followed him into the store.

The smell of spices and dry goods filled his nose, and then the realization that Mr. Brown was not behind the counter like usual. He scanned the store, which was rather empty at this time of day, and spotted the older man in the back, talking to none other than Emma Cook.

"Good morning, Elizabeth, Mr. Baxter. You two have perfect timing," Emma said with a wide smile when she saw them.

"What do you mean?" Elizabeth asked.

"Well, I was just telling Mr. Brown here about your dresses and how much the women of the town would enjoy them."

"And I was just telling Mrs. Cook that I've been looking to expand into a small space upstairs but hadn't done it yet because I had nothing to fill the extra space up there with. I'll need to see your dresses, of course, but if they are as good as Mrs. Cook says, I'd like to discuss sharing the space with you."

"Really?" Elizabeth's voice came out in a squeak, and Carl couldn't help but grin.

"Really. I know that you don't have start-up money at the moment, but once you get settled, I'll expect rent payment and a cut of the profits, of course, but I think this could be good for both of us."

Beside him, Carl felt Elizabeth stiffen. Surely, she hadn't expected to keep all the profits, had she?

"This could be a great first step," he said softly to her.

She nodded, reached into her bag and unrolled the bundle of carefully wrapped dresses and fabrics. Mr. Brown examined each piece in turn, his sharp eyes lingering on the fine stitching and intricate lace.

"These are quite lovely," he said at last. "I could see them selling very well if you are agreeable to the terms."

"That's fantastic, Elizabeth," Emma said, hugging her. "I knew it would work out, and I'm going to be your very first client."

"But you already sew," Elizabeth said.

"Not like you do, and there's another dance coming soon that I would love to have a new dress for."

As the women chatted, Carl pulled Mr. Brown to the side to verify that he was doing this of his own free will and not simply because of Emma's suggestion. Having grown up with the woman, he knew how persuasive she could be.

"Do you really think this could work? Her dresses?"

Mr. Brown shrugged. "I am not a woman, but I believe if Mrs. Cook says there is a need then she will eventually sell her creations. I cannot guarantee you how quickly it will happen, but I will keep the rent low for her."

"Thank you. I can't thank you enough for taking a chance on her."

Mr. Brown looked back at the women. "If this ends up working out, she'll be helping me just as much. Eventually, this town will grow enough to need another store and I'll need everything I can to remain competitive. This could be just the thing." He clapped Carl on the shoulder before walking back toward the women. "If you have a dress you don't mind leaving here, we'll put it in the window. Then you can set up upstairs tomorrow after I move the current stuff out."

"Do you need help with that?" Elizabeth asked. "Perhaps I could help you and then set up the area today. That is if you can spare me for a time?" She turned her questioning eyes on Carl.

His first instinct was to tell her he did need her. After all, helping around the farm was part of what he'd been looking for when he placed his ad, but he was the one encouraging her to do this and he'd known she would need to spend some time in town to make a shop work. He couldn't very well tell her now that she had to leave with him. "I can spare you today, but I do need to get back to work. Is there a time that would work for me to be back?"

"I can bring her," Emma said. "I have the wagon today since I am working at the clinic, so I'll bring her home."

"The clinic?" Elizabeth asked. "Are you a nurse?"

Emma chuckled and smiled as she shook her head slightly. "I guess some would say that though I've had no formal training. My father is Doc Moore."

"Oh, I didn't know. You must have grown up learning then."

"Something like that."

"Emma's a great help to her father," Carl said and then he nearly kicked himself when he saw Emma's eyes widen and realized he'd used her first name. It was hard getting used to her being married again, but deciding correcting himself would draw even more attention to the faux pas, he let it slide and turned to Elizabeth, squeezing her hand. "Are you fine riding back with Mrs. Cook?"

"I am, thank you."

Carl breathed a sigh of relief that Elizabeth hadn't seemed to notice his slip of the tongue as he headed back to the wagon. He should probably tell her about his history with Emma before too much longer. In fact, there was much more he wanted to say to her about everything, but it could wait for this evening when it was just the two of them.

CHAPTER 15
Elizabeth

E lizabeth couldn't wait to check out the space upstairs. Yes, it was out of the way, but it would be more private that way and surely he would be okay if she put out signs. "Can I see the space upstairs? Help you start moving things?" Elizabeth asked as Carl left the store.

"Well." Mr. Brown glanced upstairs and then surveyed the area for a minute as if he wasn't sure where he had planned to put the stuff from upstairs, causing Elizabeth to wonder if he really had been wanting to expand or if Emma had convinced him. "Sure. I think we can move the fabric and sewing materials up with you which will give me a little extra room down here. It's quite a mess up there though."

"I don't mind," Elizabeth said. Hard work that reaped benefits never seemed like work at all.

"And I can help for a bit," Emma added. "Pa has the clinic until two."

"Let's see what we can do then," Mr. Brown said, leading the way up the stairs. They were narrow and a little rickety but they managed to hold their weight.

The upstairs was also where Mr. Brown lived, so the available area wasn't very big, and it was filled with boxes.

"I guess we'll take these boxes downstairs and I'll go through them later. Then we can see about moving the fabric up here."

Elizabeth had no idea if this area would be large enough to hold the fabric let alone her dress designs and herself, but it was worth a shot and she could always move into another area if she grew. "Let's get going then."

Bending down, she grabbed one of the boxes, trying to balance it in her arms as she made her way back to the stairs. Emma and Mr. Brown followed suit and before long, they had created quite the stack in the corner of his store.

"I've got to head back to the clinic," Emma said as they dropped the last box, "but I'll come get you when we close."

"Thank you for everything." Elizabeth didn't know what Emma had said to Mr. Brown, but she was almost sure that the man wouldn't have agreed without Emma's convincing.

"Of course." Emma smiled and waved goodbye and Elizabeth turned to Mr. Brown.

"Do you have a broom? I'd like to sweep up there before we start bringing the fabric up."

The man nodded and then glanced around the store. "I'll get you a broom, but I'm afraid you're on your own after this. I have a store to run after all."

"Of course. I'm happy to do the rest and stay out of your hair."

Broom in hand, she climbed the stairs once again and then swept up the small space. When she was finished, she leaned back and surveyed the area. It was small, but perhaps the fabric could go against the wall to the left. That would leave enough room for a small table for her to cut fabric on and two chairs. It left no room to hang designs, but Mr. Brown had said she could put them in the front window. And it was hers. She needed to remember that.

She made her way back down the stairs, returned the broom, and then began grabbing the fabric. As she did, she heard muted voices coming from the front of the store. She looked up, trying to see if it was Emma who had returned, though it felt entirely too early. However, the woman talking to Mr. Brown was not Emma. It was a woman she didn't recognize, and though she didn't want to eavesdrop, she couldn't help overhearing a few words.

"Her name is Elizabeth Baxter. She married Carl."

"And you're giving her space in your store?" Disdain dripped from the woman's voice.

"Mrs. Cook said that women would be interested in her dress designs, so we'll see how it goes."

The woman laughed. "She must not know."

Not know? Not know what? And was the she referring to herself or to Emma? Who was this woman? At that moment, one of the bolts of fabric fell from her arms and into a small display, knocking it over. The commotion halted the conversation happening up front, and when Elizabeth glanced up again, the woman was gone. She wondered who she was and what exactly she'd been talking about.

Before Mr. Brown could say anything to her, Elizabeth cleaned up the mess and headed upstairs with the bolts of fabric. It took her a few more trips, but finally she had everything she needed upstairs to begin setting up the display. When it was finished, she stepped back, wiping a small sheen of sweat from her brow. It wasn't perfect, but she thought it looked decent, and once she got a table and chairs in, it would be even better.

The sound of footsteps on the creaky stairs caused her to turn, and she smiled when she saw Emma's face come into view.

"Elizabeth, this looks amazing," Emma said as she crested the stairs.

"Thank you. It still needs a little work, but I think it will get there."

"I agree, and I can't wait until you fill it with women ordering from you. I have a feeling you will make a name for yourself."

Emma's words caused Elizabeth's smile to falter. She didn't want to make a name for herself - well, she did, but she didn't because that would make it easier for Jacob to find her. "Oh, I don't need all that." She waved her hand dismissively. "Just making the local women happy will be enough for me."

"I have no doubt you will do that. I'm finished at the clinic so are you ready to head back?"

Elizabeth nodded and the women descended the stairs once more. "Shall I come in tomorrow, Mr. Brown?"

The older man shrugged. "I don't know if you'll have any clients by tomorrow, but you're welcome to. I'll try to remember to hang the dress you left in the window and we'll see what it does."

"Thank you." Of course leaving one of her dresses here meant she'd have to make another for herself, but it would give her something to do until she had customers. "Oh, and Mr. Brown, who was the woman that was here earlier? I don't believe I've met her yet, and I wanted to see if she might be interested in a dress or lessons." Elizabeth tried to play the question off nonchalantly but she was dying of curiosity. Even more than the woman's name, she wanted to know what the woman thought she ought to know but she couldn't very well ask Mr. Brown that.

Mr. Brown lifted an eyebrow as if trying to decide if that was really the motivation for her question, but he answered. "That was Miss Johnson. I'm sure Mrs. Cook can tell you more about her than I can."

Elizabeth glanced over at Emma who shifted uncomfortably. She would ask her friend about the woman but not here. "Thank you. I'll see you tomorrow." She waved to Mr. Brown and then stepped out of the entrance nearly colliding with a man who stood by the doorway. "Oh, I'm so sorry."

"You can't keep prospecting the same cave over and over again," the man said, hardly looking at her. "You need to find someplace new."

"I'm sorry?" Elizabeth asked.

Emma took her arm and led her away from the man who had now begun to smack his forehead with the palm of his hand. "Don't mind him," Emma whispered softly, "That's Christian Turner. He fought in the Civil War and it messed him up a little. He's always talking to himself about prospecting for gold."

"Oh." Elizabeth looked back at the man as they stepped away from the store. "Is there even gold around here?"

Emma chuckled. "If there is, no one has found any yet."

"That's so sad. Has he been like this long?"

"As long as he's been here," Emma said. "He's a kind man when he's in his right mind, but recently that seems to be fewer and fewer times. He was gone for a couple of months, prospecting I guess, and when he came back, his spells were much worse."

"Can anything be done for him?"

Emma sighed and shook her head. "Not that we know of. My father looked him over but can't find a reason for the spells."

Elizabeth's heart broke for the man who seemed so lonely. She knew what it was like to be alone, and she wouldn't wish that on anyone. "That's such a shame. What about Miss Johnson? Can you tell me about her?"

Emma stiffened slightly and chewed on her lip. "Miss Johnson is... Rebecca, the woman we told you about. Her best friend was Pauline. She's a good woman, but, like the rest of us, she is only human and therefore has flaws. Kindness is something she struggles with."

Elizabeth climbed into the wagon. "Oh, that's right."

Had Rebecca been referencing Pauline when she asked Mr. Brown if Elizabeth knew? That didn't make sense though because why would Elizabeth, a newcomer to town, be upset about a marriage that happened before she arrived? And how would Rebecca even know that Elizabeth knew Kate? She must have heard wrong. That was the only thing that made sense.

CHAPTER 16

Carl

Carl did his best to freshen up before the wagon reached the house. He'd spent the day working, but he'd stopped a little early in order to make dinner for Elizabeth. While that was normally her job, he wanted to do something to celebrate her getting her own business set up. He knew it would take her away from the farm, but he'd seen the light in her eye when Mr. Brown offered a piece of his store. If he could make that light remain, it would be worth it for him.

As soon as Emma pulled the wagon to a stop, he held out his hand to help Elizabeth down. "How did it go today?"

"Well, I didn't get any customers yet, besides Emma," she said, smiling up at the other woman, "but I got the area set up and Emma promised to help me spread the word."

"We'll be having a social soon, so I know there are some women who will be looking for a new dress or some help in the sewing department," Emma said.

"Sounds like an eventful day then." Carl grinned at Elizabeth, delighting in the glow that graced her cheeks. "Thank you for bringing her back, Mrs. Cook."

"Happy to help. You have a great evening." And with that, Emma flicked the reins and the horses surged forward.

"I suppose I better get cleaned up so I can make you dinner," Elizabeth said as she began to walk toward the homestead.

"Cleaned up, yes, but I made dinner tonight." He hooked his fingers in his belt loops and grinned at her.

She stopped and turned wide eyes at him. "You made dinner?"

He shrugged. "I mean it won't be as tasty as the ones you've made for the last week, but I thought I would surprise you tonight."

"That is so sweet of you, Carl, but I promise that I won't let this job interfere with my duties here."

"Hey." He grabbed her hands and placed them against his chest. "A marriage is a partnership. I wanted a partner to share life with and I'm okay if that means that sometimes I make a less than appealing dinner so that you can do something you love."

Elizabeth smiled and stepped closer to close the distance between them. "I don't know how I got so lucky finding your ad in the paper when I did."

"I do. God's touch is all over it."

"I believe you might be right about that."

At that, Carl pulled Elizabeth closer and placed his lips upon hers. He kept them gentle though his emotions wanted to deepen the kiss. He wanted to move at her pace, but he longed to have her become a partner in the way God intended.

"We better get inside and enjoy your food before it gets cold," Elizabeth said when she pulled back from the kiss, and though he wanted to protest, he was delighted to see her flushed cheeks and wild eyes that he was sure not only mirrored his own but betrayed how much she had enjoyed the kiss.

"Indeed Mrs. Baxter. I suppose we better."

The dinner was a simple stew, but Elizabeth didn't complain, and after dinner, she curled up next to him on the sofa while he read from the Bible. When he was finished with the chapter, he closed the Bible and took her hands. He rubbed his thumb across the back of her hands, enjoying the silky smoothness of her skin.

"I'm really glad that God sent you to me."

Elizabeth's breath stilled and she glanced down at their hands before looking back up at him. "I am too."

Trying to keep from rushing, Carl pulled her closer until his lips were on hers again. He had kissed Emma when they were courting, but that had been ages ago, and he did not remember it feeling this nice.

When the kiss ended, Elizabeth pressed her lips together and pulled back. "Carl, I... I'm enjoying being your wife, but I'm not ready yet. I'm sorry."

Carl shook his head and swallowed the sigh threatening to billow through his lips. "Don't be sorry. It takes time, and I will be patient." He wanted to be patient, but it was getting more challenging by the day. They might be done reading for the night, but he was clearly going to need to spend more time in prayer tonight.

She squeezed his hands before rising from the couch. "Thank you. I'm going to retire tonight before..." A soft pink bloomed on her cheeks and she shook her head as if words had failed her. "Good night."

"Good night." He watched her walk into the bedroom and close the door before sighing and rubbing his hands down his face. "Lord, I'm not sure who needs it, but either work on her heart or work on mine."

CHAPTER 17
Elizabeth

E lizabeth couldn't help smiling as she dressed the next morning. Not only would today be her first official day at her store, but she'd had such a pleasant night with Carl last night that everything felt like it was falling into place. She could still feel the gentle touch of his lips on hers, and though she hadn't invited him to share the bed, she'd been close. It was simply a matter of time now.

She opened the bedroom door quietly in case he was still sleeping, but the couch was empty. The coffee was on the stove though so she knew he was up. Had he started his chores already? The thought made her a little sad. She'd been looking forward to seeing him this morning and maybe receiving another kiss. But, he wouldn't start chores without breakfast, would he? Surely not. Yesterday, he hadn't had help, but he couldn't be that far behind. Could he?

She glanced around for any sign that he'd already eaten,

but other than the freshly-made coffee, there was nothing. So where was he? It didn't matter. She would warm up the bread and have breakfast ready for him whenever he came in.

The door opened a few minutes later, and he stepped in, smiling softly at her. "Good morning. I trust you slept well."

"I did, thank you."

He nodded, closed the door behind him, and crossed the room to where she was standing. As he stepped closer to her to grab the coffee urn, a shiver of delight raced down her spine. There was such a masculine energy radiating from him that she longed for him to hold her in his arms again.

"I saddled a horse for you today as I figure you'll be wanting to go into town again," he said.

"Oh, thank you." Elizabeth was surprised. Not that he had saddled up the horse, but that he'd done it first thing without her having to ask. "I was hoping to head there after breakfast, but I should be back earlier today to work in the garden as well."

"Very good." He smiled at her and then leaned in and placed a quick kiss on her lips. It was over too quickly, but Elizabeth knew he had work to do. Longer kisses were probably saved for free time in the evening.

They sat down for breakfast and then after she'd cleaned up, Elizabeth put together a lunch, gathered some material to work on a dress at the store, and headed out to the barn. A chestnut mare was tied to the post outside and Carl was waiting to help her mount up.

"Have you ridden before?" he asked as he untied the mare.

"I have. It's been a few years, but I think I remember." Riding lessons had been one of the few things her father had splurged on for her as a child. There were still a lot of people who owned horses in Chicago though many in the city had given them up due to the recent addition of street-cars, something Elizabeth doubted would show up in Sage Creek for a while yet.

"Good to know. This here is Brownie. She's a good girl, so you shouldn't have any issues with her."

Elizabeth nodded, and before placing her foot in the stir-rup, she put her fabric and lunch into the saddlebag to free up her hands, then grabbed her dress and swung up onto the saddle.

"You remember how to get to town?" Carl asked.

Elizabeth replayed the trips in her head. She felt confident she could find her way. "I think so. I'll be fine."

"Okay, just stay on this path and watch yourself in the high brush."

He didn't say it, but Elizabeth remembered the brush they had to pass through just before reaching the town. It was tall enough and thick enough for someone to hide in, and the thought gave her pause. Was he worried about someone attacking her? Surely not. He was probably just being cautious. After all, she was a woman, unfamiliar with the area, traveling alone. But she would keep her guard up. She always did. "I will."

"Have fun then."

Elizabeth flicked the reins to get the horse moving, and soon the homestead was just a speck behind her. The first part of the trip was quiet and peaceful. Elizabeth lifted her face as the warm sun beat down, spreading warmth and life, but as she entered the brush, the mood changed. A chill crept up Elizabeth's back. She glanced around, but she could see no one hiding in the brush. Could they be completely camouflaged?

Flicking the reins, she urged the horse to go a little faster, but only when she reached the general store did her discomfort lessen. The feeling of eyes watching her lingered, but there were people milling about the town that made her feel safer. She tied up the mare, grabbed her items, and hurried into the store.

"Good morning, Mr. Brown," she called as she entered.

He looked up from the shelf he was stocking. "Good morning. I didn't expect you this early, but I placed your dress in the window. Come tell me how it looks."

Though she had seen the dress when she arrived, she followed him to the display. "It looks amazing. Thank you for doing this."

He rubbed his chin as he surveyed his work. "You're right. It does look amazing, and I'm sure it will draw customers in."

She smiled. "I hope so, but now that one of my dresses is unavailable to wear for a time, I need to make a new one. However, please let me know if I can help you in any way."

"Thank you. I will."

As he returned to stocking the shelves, she made her

way upstairs, but when she reached the top, she realized she still had no table or chair, so after dropping her bag, she returned downstairs to see what she could scrounge up.

"I'm sorry to bother you, Mr. Brown, but do you have an extra chair and a small table that I can use upstairs?"

Mr. Brown paused his stocking to look around the store. "I'm afraid I don't have a table, but there is a chair in the back room that you could use."

"Thank you." She followed Mr. Brown's directions to the back room. It was small and clearly held his extra supplies, so it took her a few minutes to find the chair he was talking about. After moving the supplies covering it, she took the chair upstairs and then pulled out her fabric.

A few hours later, she heard footsteps on the stairs. She glanced up to see the dark-haired woman from yesterday. Rebecca something or other. "Hello, are you looking for a dress?"

"Maybe, but I'm more curious about you. Mr. Brown says you're new to town." She smiled, but there was something off about it, as if it didn't quite reach her eyes.

"I am. I came out here from Chicago."

"Oh? Do you have family here?"

Heat climbed Elizabeth's neck. "Well, I have married Carl Baxter. He is my family now, but before that, no. My family all lived in Chicago, but sadly, they've all passed away."

Rebecca's face folded in what Elizabeth assumed she thought was compassion though it came off more like mock sympathy. "Oh, you poor dear. Maybe that's why Emma didn't tell you. At least, I assume she didn't."

Though Elizabeth was sure she didn't want to hear whatever Rebecca was about to say, she also couldn't help but ask. "Tell me what?"

Rebecca glanced down at the general store area and lowered her voice. "I'm not sure I should say anything. It's probably not my place."

No, it probably wasn't, but now Elizabeth had to know. If it concerned her, she needed to know. Right? "If it involves me, then I should hear it."

A mischievous glint sparkled in Rebecca's eyes. "Well, it involves you in a roundabout way, but if I were you, I would want to know that my husband had courted and proposed to Mrs. Emma Cook - before she married William Cook, that is."

"What?" Elizabeth felt like she had been punched in the stomach. "That can't be true."

"Oh, but it is." Now that she'd piqued Elizabeth's curiosity, Rebecca leaned closer as if sharing a scandalous secret. "They were childhood friends and he proposed to her before she met her first husband, Joseph. She said no, but he proposed again when Joseph was killed. Then when she began courting William, he found out that William had been the man in charge of getting Joseph killed, and they had a big argument about it."

"Why are you telling me this?" Elizabeth asked.

Rebecca shrugged and leaned back, once again looking as if she couldn't care less. "Because I would want to know what kind of man I married and if there were ulterior motives behind Emma's help. After all, Carl clearly loved Emma. Perhaps he still does."

Could that be true? Elizabeth thought back to the encounters with Emma. Carl hadn't seemed like he was in love with the woman, but there had been a few instances where they'd exchanged glances as if sharing an unspoken message. Could he still have feelings for Emma? If so, why would he bring her here? Was it an attempt to make Emma jealous? Or simply in hopes that he would get over her? And what did that mean for Elizabeth? He'd been so kind and gentle towards her. And they'd kissed. In fact, she had been close to inviting him to share the bed with her last night. She supposed she was glad that she hadn't now.

She looked back at Rebecca. Emma and the other women had told her that Rebecca had been unkind to Kate at first, but that had been because of Pauline. And Emma had said that kindness was something Rebecca struggled with, but knowing what she did now, could she trust Emma's words? Why would Rebecca want to hurt Elizabeth? Although maybe it wasn't Elizabeth. Maybe she wanted to hurt Emma or Carl. But could Rebecca be right? Could Carl still love Emma? The thought made Elizabeth sick to her stomach, but she knew she'd have to find out the truth. "Well, thank you for telling me. I think you're wrong though. I've seen Carl and Emma interact, and they don't seem like they're in love."

A small smug grin tugged at Rebecca's lips. "Think what you want. I just know I wouldn't put up with it if it was me, but then again, I guess you have nowhere else to go, so maybe you have to. Anyway, I'd keep an eye open if I were you."

And then before Elizabeth could ask if Rebecca needed a dress or if she'd just come to gossip, the girl turned around and left, leaving Elizabeth confused and bewildered. Was Rebecca telling the truth or trying to stir the pot? Unless the woman was like this with everyone, the latter made little sense. Rebecca didn't know Elizabeth and couldn't guarantee she would go sharing the news, so her words being the truth made far more sense. Unfortunately, it raised even more questions. If it was the truth, why hadn't Carl or Emma told her? She supposed she could understand Emma not saying anything as it sounded like Carl had been the ones with feelings that Emma hadn't reciprocated. But why would Carl introduce her to Emma knowing they had a history? And why would he not disclose that history? He had to know she would find out sooner or later. Deciding she wouldn't feel better until she found out, Elizabeth laid down the dress she'd been working on and went in search of Emma.

Though she'd never been to the clinic, Elizabeth found it easily thanks to Mr. Brown's directions. She knocked lightly on the door and pushed it open when Emma smiled and waved from inside.

"Elizabeth, so good to see you. Have you had lunch? I was just about to eat and would love for you to join me."

In the wake of Rebecca's visit, Elizabeth had forgotten all

about eating. "I left my food back at the store. I really just came to ask you a question."

Emma's brow wrinkled slightly, but she nodded. "Okay, what is it?"

"Did you and Carl court?"

The color drained from Emma's face, and her smile faded. "Who told you that?"

"Rebecca. She just left the general store. Is it true?"

Emma sighed. "It is, but it's not what you think, Elizabeth. Carl and I grew up together, and as you can tell, there aren't a lot of women in this town. Carl thought we belonged together, and we were good friends so we did court for a time, but I didn't feel the way he did. Then Joseph entered my life and I fell for him."

"But Rebecca said he proposed again just months ago. She claims that you're still in love or, at least, that Carl is still in love with you."

Emma shook her head. "Rebecca is a hurting woman who doesn't always think before she speaks. Carl is no longer in love with me, if he ever was. I think because we grew up together, he thought we would be good as husband and wife, but we wouldn't have been. Maybe it took Carl a little longer to accept that, but he did, so Rebecca not only spoke out of turn, but I'm afraid she didn't speak the whole truth."

Elizabeth chewed the inside of her lip. She wanted to believe Emma, but how could she really be sure that Carl didn't still love her. What if putting out the ad had been a desperate attempt from Carl to get over Emma?

"I hear what you're saying, but how do I trust that Carl is no longer in love with you?"

Emma smiled softly. "The best way I can think of is to ask him. A good marriage is built on communication."

Elizabeth supposed that was true, but could she trust Carl to tell her the truth? There was only one way to find out.

CHAPTER 18

Carl

It was barely after midday when Carl heard a horse approaching. It had to be Elizabeth, but he certainly hadn't expected her so early. Still, he'd be grateful for the help. Setting down his tools, he walked toward the barn to meet her. When she reached him, she pulled on the reins and then dismounted, but she wasn't smiling like she had been yesterday. He wondered if something had happened in town.

"Is everything alright? Did something happen?"

She tilted her head at him and folded her arms across her chest. Anger radiated off her like the hormones of an animal in heat, but he had no idea what she was riled up about. "You could say that. You could have told me that you were in love with Emma and that you proposed to her, so that I wasn't blindsided with the information."

Carl's mouth fell open as shock and then anger filled him. "Well, first off, I'm not in love with Emma, and I never mentioned us courting because I didn't think it mattered. That was months ago. And who told you anyway?" He couldn't imagine Emma telling her. Not only was she not spiteful like that, but his feelings for her had been a source of discomfort for her. One he knew she'd rather forget.

"Not that it matters, but a woman named Rebecca told me. I should have heard it from you though." She pointed a finger at his chest. "Do you know how much of a fool I feel like knowing that the whole town knows you are in love with another woman?"

Carl narrowed his eyes at her and struggled to maintain his urge to yell. He was angry at Rebecca, who had once been a kind and caring girl but had changed after Pauline's death, but he was also irritated with Elizabeth. She had no right to raise her voice at him. "Rebecca should not have said anything. It wasn't her place and it's in the past."

"In the past?" The pitch of Elizabeth's voice lifted as she threw her arms out. "How far in the past is it, Carl? Both Rebecca and Emma told me you courted before her first marriage and then you proposed again before this second marriage."

Carl took a deep breath to keep from yelling back at her. "Now wait just a minute. There is truth to those statements but there were also circumstances that you don't know about."

"Yes, I heard about those. You were friends, you figured you belonged together, her husband had just died... but how can I be sure you no longer have feelings for her? Especially when Rebecca claimed you tried to discourage Emma's relationship with William. What kind of man does that?"

Carl sighed and rubbed a hand down his face. She was the one yelling, yet he felt like he was the one on trial, and though he wished he had handled the situation with Emma and William differently, Elizabeth had no right to judge him for it. "Look, that was not my finest hour. I will admit that I told Emma what I did in hopes of getting her to send William away, but I also thought I was protecting her. She deserved to know William's role in Joseph's death."

"And what was William's role in Joseph's death?"

"Well, that's a long story, but the short of it is that he was in charge of a group of men, Joseph included, who were sent after an outlaw. William thought they had the man secured, but he managed to grab a gun and shoot Joseph and another man. I felt that Emma deserved to know that before she got involved with him, but that was a mistake."

Her eyes narrowed to slits. "So you felt she deserved to know in that situation, but that I didn't deserve to know your history with her?" She shook her head and then handed him the reins before turning toward the homestead. "You should have told me."

Carl blew out a frustrated breath as he quickly tied the horse up and followed her. Words were not his specialty and they were certainly failing him today. "I'm not doing a good job explaining it, but please let me try."

She glared at him as she pulled open the door, but he wasn't going to let her leave it like this. They may not have a marriage born out of love - though he thought they'd been getting close - but his mother had always told him never to go to bed angry and he wasn't about to start now.

"Look, Emma and I grew up together and yes, I thought we were going to get married, but then Joseph, her first husband showed up and I could tell that they shared something she and I never did."

"I know. She told me that, so why didn't you marry someone else then?" Elizabeth asked as she pulled out a chair and sat down.

Though he wanted to sit down and reason with her, he felt that she was using the table as a barrier between them and he wanted to honor her feelings, so he leaned against the wall. "There weren't a lot of options. In case you hadn't noticed, the men outnumber the women here."

"You could have asked Sarah or Rebecca. They've both been here a while, right?"

"Yes, I suppose," he said, wondering what she was getting at, "but both of them are much younger and I don't think they were of marrying age the first time Emma married. Regardless, I didn't know them like I knew Emma. When Joseph was killed, I figured it meant Emma and I were supposed to be together, but I think I was more in love with the idea of Emma than the woman she'd grown to be. We never clicked romantically, and when she married William, I knew it was time to move on.

"Look, I am sorry that I didn't tell you about Emma, and I'm certainly sorry that Rebecca did." He took a breath and rubbed his hand across the back of his neck. "I don't know what her purpose in telling you that was, but I am no longer in love with Emma, if I ever truly was, and when I said "I do" to you, I made a vow to you that I intend to keep."

Elizabeth stared at him for another few beats before sighing. "I want to believe you, but I may need some time to process this."

She might need time? What about him? He'd thought they'd become friends and were on their way to a mutual affection, but now he wondered if he'd made a terrible mistake. This was the second time she'd raised her voice at him, and he wasn't sure how to address the issue. He took a deep breath. "I think we should both take some time. We'll talk later."

"Perhaps."

Her tone was chilly, but Carl felt cool towards her as well. All of the progress they had made over the last few weeks seemed to have disappeared in one argument, and he would have to pray that they could find a way to overcome it. Pray that he could find the right words to say to her. Pray that she would understand. He didn't know why he hadn't told Elizabeth about Emma, other than it hadn't been a big deal to him, but he supposed he could see how it would be to her, especially getting blindsided with it like she did.

Exiting the cabin, he took care of Brownie and then finished his chores, talking to God all the while. There was so much more to being married than he'd thought about, even thought to ask Jesse about, but he was sure that God would help him learn.

When he came in to supper after the sun had set, Elizabeth had the food ready, but the atmosphere was still cooler than it had been yesterday. He decided not to push the issue though and to let her talk when she was ready, so he took his seat at the table, complimented her on the meal, and bowed his head to pray.

When supper was finished, he retired to the couch in the living room to read from the Bible as he did every night, and though Elizabeth joined him, she sat in the chair instead of joining him on the couch. Still, she listened as she stitched something and that was enough for tonight.

When he finished reading though, the silence in the room pressed down on him, suffocating him, and he couldn't help but address the elephant in the room. "I've thought about what you said earlier, and you're right, I should have told you about Emma. To be honest, I think I didn't because I'm ashamed of how I handled the situation and I didn't want you to know about it, to look at me differently, but I've also apologized to both Emma and William, so to me, it really is in the past. However, I need to know if this is how you handle issues and how you plan to handle them in the future because I'm not really okay with that. I'm hoping for a partner, someone I can face challenges with together, but that's going to require some different communication skills."

She glanced up from her sewing before sighing and putting it down beside her. "You're right. I should not have raised my voice at you." She offered a small, tight smile. "I might have forgotten to mention that I'm rather independent. I'm used to looking out for myself and sometimes I forget that a marriage is a partnership. I will try to remember in the future. Tonight, however, I think I'm going to retire."

Carl watched as she walked into the bedroom and shut the door. He wasn't sure what to make of their conversation. On one hand, he felt like perhaps things had improved, that they'd at least come to an understanding, but on the other hand, it still felt like an ocean lay between them.

He stretched out on the couch and stared at the ceiling. "God, I believe that You put us together for some reason. Please give me the knowledge and patience to deal with these situations." His prayer sent, he closed his eyes and hoped that tomorrow would be a better day.

CHAPTER 19

Elizabeth

E lizabeth's ire softened somewhat by morning. Carl's words had played over and over in her head as she'd tossed late into the night. Finally, she'd been forced to admit that she hadn't acted in the best way either. Yes, Carl should have told her, but she couldn't expect the man to have had no past before her, and now that she was married, she did need to work on being a partner instead of only thinking about herself, so she'd prayed for God's help in that area and finally drifted off to sleep.

Though she did still worry that Carl's feelings for Emma weren't entirely gone, she had exchanged vows, and that meant something to her. It seemed to mean something to him as well, so as she dressed for the day, she decided to make an effort to forgive him.

"Good morning," he said as she opened the bedroom door.

She noticed he made no move to kiss her this morning

like he had yesterday, and she wasn't sure if she was relieved or hurt. "Good morning."

"Will you be going into town again today?"

"If that's agreeable with you. I'd like to continue working on the dress I started and also see if there's a way to advertise my services to the women."

He issued a single nod. "I was simply asking to see if you needed the horse saddled again today."

"Oh, yes, thank you."

He looked at her a moment longer before dropping his gaze back to his Bible and continuing his reading. Elizabeth hesitated only a moment before preparing breakfast. She didn't like the uncomfortable tension that filled the room, but she knew a lot of it was her fault. If she told him she forgave him and understood, she had no doubt that the mood would lighten, but she wasn't sure she was ready to do that yet, so instead she tried to ignore the tension as she prepared breakfast.

After the meal, she cleaned the dishes and then headed out to the barn. As promised, Carl had Brownie saddled and ready for her, and her hurt dissipated a tiny bit more. He didn't have to do this for her. He could have told her she was being unreasonable and to just do it herself, but he hadn't. Perhaps he had been telling the truth that he no longer had feelings for Emma. At the very least, it seemed that he was telling the truth that he wanted to make this marriage work.

"Thank you," she said as she took the reins and swung up on the horse. She opened her mouth to say more, but decided against it. She still needed more time. They could talk then.

Elizabeth enjoyed the quiet ride into town until she felt it again. The hairs on her arms stood on end, and her senses prickled. She glanced around, trying to appear unconcerned, but the feeling of being watched unnerved her. If someone was watching her though, they were doing a good job of hiding and waiting because she heard nothing out of the ordinary - no breathing, no movement of leaves, no snapping of twigs. She was glad the town was visible, but the eerie feeling didn't leave her even when she reached the general store.

A large man with a deputy star upon his chest leaned against the post staring at her. She'd never seen him before, but he looked at her as if he knew her and his gaze was cold and hard. She dismounted and approached the post warily. "Is there an issue at the store, Deputy?"

"Not at the store, no, but there is an issue at the clinic."

Elizabeth's eyes widened, and she glanced back toward the clinic. "The clinic? Is Emma all right?"

He folded his arms across his chest and narrowed his eyes at her. "Mrs. Cook and her father are both fine, physically, but it appears that someone broke into the clinic last night."

Elizabeth gasped. "Why would anyone do such a thing?" Then her eyes widened as she realized this deputy, a man she'd never met, must be questioning her because he thought she was to blame. "You don't think I had anything to do with it, do you?"

He studied her for a minute before standing to his full height. "Well, I don't know. It has been brought to my attention that you and Mrs. Cook had a disagreement yesterday."

"A disagreement, yes, but I have no reason to break into her father's clinic or steal from her. Plus, I went home to my husband, Carl Baxter, afterwards and was there all night. You can ask him."

The deputy nodded and fixed her with a pointed stare. "Oh I will, don't you worry. I know you're new here, but we don't take kindly to people stealing from our own."

The door to the general store opened then and Mr. Brown stepped out. "That's enough, Deputy Masterson. You are keeping this woman from getting to work."

Deputy Masterson rubbed his chin for a moment before agreeing. "Very well, but I'll be keeping an eye on you, Mrs. Baxter."

Elizabeth waited until the deputy had sauntered away before turning to Mr. Brown. "Thank you. I don't know why he would think I had anything to do with a robbery."

"I do. This is a small town and word spreads quickly. I heard Christian telling everyone in the saloon about your disagreement with Mrs. Cook last night. Now, it's none of my business, but I can tell you that I've known both Carl and Mrs. Cook for years. While it is true that he was sweet on her at one time, I have always found him to be a man of his word, so if he tells you that there's nothing there anymore, I'd believe him."

Elizabeth nodded. "I'm trying to, but I was a little caught

off guard when Rebecca told me yesterday. Neither Carl nor Emma had said anything about their history."

Mr. Brown stepped into the store, holding the door open for her. "I believe it's because it was just that - history. When Mrs. Cook remarried again, Carl accepted that, and that's when he placed the ad. Now I know he knew love wouldn't happen right out of the gate, but he also had hope that it would grow with whatever woman God sent his way."

Elizabeth sighed. "He is being very kind about all of this."

Mr. Brown stopped and looked her in the eye, his gaze steady as if he was trying to convey his words through it. "That should tell you everything then."

Yes, it probably should. She'd thought that this morning but hadn't said anything and now she felt guilty. She would tell Carl she was sorry as soon as she returned home, but before then, there was someone else she needed to speak to. "I'll talk to him today, but I should probably go check on Emma, let her know that I had nothing to do with this."

Mr. Brown nodded and smiled as if his work was finished. "I'm sure she knows, but a kind word never hurts. Just be careful. Word spreads quickly in this small town, and I'm sure others will have heard the same information that Deputy Masterson did.

"Thank you, Mr. Brown. I will."

Elizabeth set down her things upstairs and then hurried over to the clinic. She waved at Emma through the window before opening the front door. "I'm so sorry, Emma. I heard from the deputy this morning that someone broke in. He seemed to think it was me, but I wanted to assure you that I had nothing to do with it. You believe me, don't you?"

Emma's mouth formed a tight smile. "I do find it hard to believe you would be capable of such a thing, but you are the only new person in town which I assume is part of why the deputy suspects you, and some might say you would have a reason to hurt me."

"Because of Carl's feelings for you?" Even though Carl had stated he no longer cared for Emma, Elizabeth still wasn't convinced that was the case, but she would never take that out on the other woman. She could not believe this was happening. Never in her life had she been so unfairly judged. "But you were right. I spoke with him, and he said he no longer has the feelings he once did. It's given us a set back, but we're both committed to making this marriage work."

"I'm glad to hear that, and it does seem a silly reason to steal from someone, but it is understandable for the deputy to have a hard time seeing who else it might be."

"Could it have been a random robber? Didn't Sarah say that's how that woman was killed?" Elizabeth tried to remember the woman's name. "The woman who Mr. Jennings was supposed to marry."

"Pauline?" Emma nodded. "It is possible, though in that case, the robbers were after the money in the bank and they did it openly. This break in happened at night when no one would be likely to see anything."

Elizabeth pursed her lips as she thought. "Well, you

certainly know the people in this town better than I do, and since I know it wasn't me, it was either a random act or someone trying to blame me." She paused and looked at Emma. "Do you think it could have been Rebecca?"

Emma's brow lifted again. "Do you really want to cast aspersions on her without proof knowing how it feels?"

Elizabeth shook her head. Emma was right. She didn't know Rebecca and therefore had no idea if the woman had told her the information out of malice or simply because she'd thought Elizabeth should know, and she certainly had no proof the woman was behind it. "No, but I do wonder why she told me about you and Carl. You said she had an issue with Kate, but does she have one with you or Carl as well?"

"Not that I'm aware of. Perhaps she really thought she was doing the right thing."

Elizabeth had her doubts about that. Rebecca had been smug about it like she'd enjoyed telling Elizabeth. "I just wish the deputy had a better option than me."

Emma stepped forward and placed her hand on Elizabeth's arm. "I understand, and I am sure the deputy and the sheriff are looking into it. Whoever is behind the break in will be brought to justice."

Elizabeth could feel the promise in those words. Emma might be saying she didn't blame her, but it seemed she had her doubts and why wouldn't she? Elizabeth was new to town and no one had a vested interest in her innocence besides Carl. If even Emma didn't believe her completely, why would the sheriff or the deputy look any further than herself? "I hope so. Thank you for at least listening to me."

"Of course. I wasn't lying when I said that I hope we can become friends."

Elizabeth smiled softly. "It seems I could definitely use friends. Is there anything I can do to help here?" Elizabeth looked around, but the clinic appeared orderly and tidy. Perhaps the break in had happened at the back?

Emma shook her head. "No, what you can do is create a beautiful poster that I can hang in here letting everyone know about your business."

Emma might have her doubts, but Elizabeth appreciated that she was willing to still help and give Elizabeth the benefit of the doubt. "That was on my list of things to do today."

"Good, so get it done, and when you have a few done, swing back by and we'll hang them together. That should quiet the town gossip as well."

Though it was not usually her nature, Elizabeth reached forward and hugged Emma. "Thank you." Then she hurried back to the general store. She had a lot to do today if she was going to finish a dress and make posters and hang them.

CHAPTER 20

Carl

Carl glanced up at the approach of thundering hooves, and his hand fell to his side where he kept his gun. That was too many horses to be Elizabeth returning, and though it hadn't happened often, there had been a few times when roving gangs of robbers had ridden through his field. The first time it had happened, he'd been woefully unprepared and nearly taken a bullet to the shoulder. Thankfully, he'd been on his horse and able to outrun them by taking a shortcut he knew about. Ever since then though, he'd taken to wearing his gun when he was far out to keep it from happening.

As soon as he recognized the men on the horses though, his hand relaxed. He didn't know what the sheriff and the deputy might want, but he wasn't in any danger. A moment later, they pulled to a stop a few feet from him.

"Afternoon, Sheriff, what can I do for you?"

"Afternoon, Carl. I wish we were here on different terms,

but we need to ask you a few questions. You recently got married, didn't you?"

Carl's brow furrowed. "I did, but what does that have to do with anything? I'm pretty sure getting married is still legal around here."

The sheriff chuckled. "It is, but your wife is not from around here. Is that correct?"

"That's true. She answered my ad and came from Chicago."

The sheriff nodded. "Do you know anything about her past there?"

"Some. I know her father died and she didn't have any family. The rest wasn't important. Are you going to tell me what's going on?"

"There's been a situation."

That got Carl's attention and adrenaline flooded his veins. "A situation? Is Elizabeth okay? Did something happen at the store?" Images of her being shot like Pauline had been filled his head and he fought the urge to jump on his horse and race into town.

The sheriff held up his hand and shook his head. "Nothing like that. Elizabeth is fine. It's Doc Moore's clinic."

"The doc's clinic? I don't understand."

"Someone broke into the clinic last night and stole some medical supplies."

Carl's jaw fell open. "And you think Elizabeth had something to do with it? My wife is not a thief." Though he didn't like it, Carl could understand their questions. Sage

Creek had seen few new people over the years, so they were a tight knit community who all knew each other, but the sheriff casting dispersions on his wife, even if they had married for the sake of convenience, didn't sit well with him.

"No one is saying that," the sheriff said, his tone taking on a placating edge, "but there has been talk of her having a disagreement with Mrs. Cook after finding out about your history. We're just checking all the boxes. Elizabeth claims she was home with you last night. Can you confirm that information?"

Carl didn't know where this line of questioning was headed, but he knew the sheriff was a good man which was the only reason he continued to answer. "Yes, sir. She was here all night."

The sheriff glanced over at the deputy and nodded. "All right, and can you confirm that no medical supplies have shown up here unexpectedly?"

Carl locked gazes with Deputy Masterson. He hadn't been exactly thrilled when James had taken over the deputy position when Jesse stepped down, but he'd had no say. It wasn't that James wasn't a decent man, but he did have a habit of jumping to conclusions before getting all the information. "I can confirm that as well."

"Very well. We'll pursue our other leads."

"What other leads?" James asked, speaking for the first time. "She is the only lead, the only one who makes sense."

"Perhaps you should check in with Miss Johnson as it seems she's the one who informed Elizabeth of my previous feelings for Mrs. Cook. Now, I don't know what she'd have against Elizabeth or Mrs. Cook or even myself, but as she inserted herself, perhaps it's worth asking."

"Will do, Carl. Thanks for your time."

Carl watched the men ride away before he returned to his job, but he couldn't help wondering about Elizabeth. Had they harassed her already? And if they had, how must she be feeling? The protective part of him wanted to ride into town and check on her, but Elizabeth had not only proven herself to be independent, she'd pushed him away when she found out about Emma. He doubted she would appreciate him riding in like some knight in shining armor trying to rescue her. No, he would just have to wait until she returned and check on her then.

It was shortly after he'd finished dinner and well before he expected her to arrive that Elizabeth returned. He could tell by the grim expression on her face that her day had not gone as well as she'd hoped.

"Are you alright?" he asked as he held out his hand to help her down.

"Just peachy. If you consider everyone in town thinking I'm a thief alright. Do you know they honestly believe I broke into Emma's clinic and stole medical supplies?"

Carl nodded and adjusted his hat. "I do, but only because the sheriff and Deputy Masterson paid me a visit earlier."

Elizabeth's eyes widened, and her expression, though he wouldn't have thought it possible, darkened. "Do you mean to tell me they rode out here to ask questions about me?"

"They did, but while they were just doing their jobs, I told them they were barking up the wrong tree."

Elizabeth sighed and brushed her hand down her skirt. "Thank you, but little good it will do me. Rebecca made sure everyone in town heard about the break in and the deputy suspecting me. Then she publicly ridiculed Emma for helping me hang signs about my business. Not that anyone will want to buy a dress from me now."

"You just have to give them time. I don't know what Rebecca's problem is, but I know that the people of this town are decent folks and when they realize you are innocent..."

"That's just it though, Carl, why do they have to realize I'm innocent? Why am I guilty first? That's not the way it's supposed to work."

Carl looked at her, wondering if she realized what she'd just said.

"What?" she asked.

"I agree that you should be innocent first, but shouldn't I have been too?"

For a second she stared at him and then he saw the realization hit. Her eyes widened and her hand flew to her mouth. "Oh my goodness, Carl, you're right. I should have talked to you and not yelled at you. I'm so sorry."

Carl smiled and stepped toward her, but he didn't touch her. Though she had apologized, he wasn't sure if she was ready to rekindle the affection they'd started. "I accept your apology, and I want you to know that the people of this town will issue the same kind of apology when they realize they've been wrong. It's a small town, Elizabeth, and most people here grew up together. They just need time to get to know you."

She pulled back her shoulders and lifted her chin in the air. "Well, I'm not going anywhere. I will not be falsely accused and run out of town." With that, she headed toward the homestead. Carl sighed. Married life was certainly harder than he'd thought it would be.

CHAPTER 21

Elizabeth

Elizabeth yawned as the light filtered in through the small bedroom window the next morning. She wasn't normally so tired in the morning, but she hadn't slept well the night before at all. The events of the day before kept replaying in her head, and she'd tossed and turned trying to figure out if she could have done anything differently. She'd come up empty, and so the prospect of another day in town didn't hold the same excitement she'd felt yesterday, but she wouldn't give up. Not only because she'd told Carl she wouldn't, but also because it wasn't in her nature.

Yawning once more, she stretched and breathed deeply, hoping the extra oxygen would wake her up. Then she pushed back the covers, placed her feet on the floor, and forced herself to begin her day.

She pulled out her blue gingham dress and put it on. It wasn't her favorite, but with one dress in the store window, one unfinished in her shop, and the others needing to be washed, it would have to do. She'd been so busy lately that she'd been neglecting the washing, but she would make sure she had time to do it this afternoon.

Carl was at his usual place at the table when she entered the kitchen and she answered his 'good morning' with a nod while she began heating the oats for breakfast.

When she set the bowl down in front of him, he grasped her hand. "I know you're struggling with all of this, Elizabeth, but God is bigger than this issue, bigger than the people in this town, and even bigger than you and me. If we trust in Him, He will guide us through this."

Elizabeth looked down at his hand holding hers, and her skin tingled from his touch. She hadn't realized how much she missed that simple human connection. And then his words registered with her, and she realized that she hadn't been talking to God. She hadn't brought this issue before Him at all. Nor had she prayed for wisdom on how to deal with the situation. Carl was right. She did need to turn her focus back to God.

"I haven't been doing a very good job of that these last few days," she said as she squeezed his hand and took her place across from him, "but I think you're right, and I'm going to try and do better."

Carl smiled. "We all stumble from time to time, but I'm delighted to hear you say that. Let's start now."

Elizabeth closed her eyes and let him pray for her, and she had to admit that she did feel a little more at peace when he finished. They finished breakfast, and then Elizabeth helped Carl saddle up Brownie. She figured she would need to learn to do it herself one day.

"Thank you," she said as they finished.

"For what?" he asked.

She stepped closer to him. "For being patient with me. For letting me follow my dreams, and for not pushing things between us to move faster. I know this probably isn't what you were hoping for, but I am trying."

He took hold of her hands again. "I would be lying if I said I wasn't looking forward to the day we have what Kate and Jesse or William and Emma do, but I've asked God for patience, and I do believe He will get us both through this."

"I hope you're right. It feels awful being accused of something I didn't do and not having people trust my word. I'm sorry that I didn't believe you at first about Emma." She pulled her hand from his to place it on his cheek. "You're a good man, Carl Baxter."

Carl placed his hand upon hers and pulled it to his chest. "And you're a good woman, Mrs. Baxter. I understand why you had a hard time trusting my words since I wasn't the one to tell you first. I hope today goes much better for you."

She smiled up at him. "I think it will." Then she lifted on her toes and brushed her lips quickly against his. It was a small gesture, but one she hoped he would understand was her peace offering and baby step towards more. Before the kiss could deepen, she pulled back and swung up onto the horse. "I'll be back later."

Carl waved as she urged the horse forward, and she was on her way. Though less jubilant today, Elizabeth had hope that things would improve for her in town. As she entered the thickest part of the brush before town though, a chill ran through her body once again. Just like yesterday and the day before, she felt like eyes were watching her. She glanced around, but there was nothing there. Or at least nothing she could see, but someone had to be watching her. She just wished she knew who. And why.

She pulled the horse to a stop in front of the general store and blinked. Her dress was gone from the window. Had someone stolen it as well? She would hate for that to be the case, but if they'd stolen from her, perhaps that would help convince the deputy and the other members of the town that she was innocent.

With her heart pounding in her chest, she tied the horse to the rail and then pulled open the door to the general store. Mr. Brown looked up as she entered and though he said nothing, she could read volumes on his face.

"No. Not again. What happened now?"

"Someone cut some fence on the Johnson's farm. A bunch of their cattle escaped. I'm sorry, but I had to take your dress out of the window, and I have to shut you down for now. Until this is all figured out."

Elizabeth's eyes burned as anger and hurt welled up inside her. "But you know I didn't do this, don't you, Mr. Brown?" Her voice trembled and she hated herself for showing emotion.

Mr. Brown sighed and shuffled around the counter toward her. "I do believe you, but I have a business to run as well. With it being the Johnson farm and your issue with

Rebecca, I'm afraid I may be one of the only ones who does. His eyes were soft with sympathy, but his words were a knife to her heart. "Hopefully it's only for a few days while they find the culprit..."

"They won't though," Elizabeth said, shaking her head. "They've already decided it's me and they probably won't look anywhere else." She couldn't believe this was happening again. How would she ever prove her innocence? If it was Rebecca trying to frame her, had she really cut her own fence just to cast the blame on Elizabeth? That seemed unlikely as lost cattle would cost her family money, but if it wasn't Rebecca, then who would do such a thing? And then a cold feeling settled in the pit of her stomach.

"What is it, Mrs. Baxter?"

Elizabeth shook her head. She wouldn't say anything until she was sure. "Nothing. Is my dress okay?"

A look of sympathy covered his face. "It's upstairs with your other things. I didn't want anything to happen to it. Now, I'm not trying to run you out, Mrs. Baxter, but the menfolk were helping Mr. Johnson round up the cattle. They'll be coming back soon and.."

"And I should be gone when they do," she finished for him.

"I'm so sorry, but they'll be wanting a word with you when they return."

Elizabeth nodded, tears pricking her eyes. She would not cry though. There was too much to do. If this was Jacob's doing, she needed to find him and stop him. Before he did something worse.

Untying her horse, she quickly swung up and headed toward the outskirts of town. If she'd felt eyes on her as she passed through the brush, maybe it was finally time to investigate it a little closer. The noise of the town, though it had been quieter today, faded behind her and the sound of chirping birds and the rustling of leaves in the gentle breeze took its place. How peaceful this place would feel if she wasn't so…

Elizabeth was flying through the air before she even had time to register what had happened. Her right shoulder hit the ground first followed by her hip and then her head. Pain shot through every nerve in her body, and she faintly heard the horse whinny and then take off running.

"No…" She was fairly certain that she uttered the word and that her hand reached out, but her head was so heavy and the light hurt her eyes. Then she felt hands on her, lifting her up. Someone had found her. They had seen her fall from the horse and were going to take her to Doc Moore, to Emma, but no, she wasn't being carried with care. She was slung over someone's shoulder.

"Careful with her. I want her alive."

Elizabeth's heart nearly stopped. She knew that voice.

Jacob.

Panic flooded her senses and she forced herself to fight through the pain. She pounded on the man's back and flailed her legs, hoping to land a solid enough kick that the man would let her down, but his grip was like iron, and her strength was no match for his.

She opened her mouth to scream, but before she could,

her head was yanked backward and a calloused hand covered her mouth. "Best come along quietly," Jacob said, his breath hot on her neck. "Unless you'd like me to rough you up a bit first."

Elizabeth whimpered against his hand, her pulse pounding in her throat. She had known Jacob was dangerous, but never had she imagined he would go this far. How had he even found her? And who was the man carrying her?

"Now, I'm going to remove my hand from your mouth, but if you scream, I'll make certain it's the last thing you do."

She was tempted to test him on that, but her head still pounded and the man holding her was too strong for her in her injured condition. It would be better to wait and see if an opportunity for escape arose when he put her down, so she kept her mouth closed. Jacob flashed a triumphant smile at her and then hollered for the man to keep going. The man began moving again, but Elizabeth had no idea where he was taking her.

She tried to gauge how long they walked, but the bouncing with every step set off the pain in her head, and she was fairly certain she blacked out a time or two. Suddenly, the man stopped moving. She raised her head to look around, but before she could, he unceremoniously dropped her onto the ground, the jolt reverberating through her body and causing her teeth to snap together. Another burst of pain exploded in her head, but she managed to get a look at the man who'd carried her. Not that it mattered as she didn't recognize him at all. No doubt Jacob had simply enlisted some unsavory help from a nearby saloon.

"I'll take my money now," the man said, his voice deep and gravelly and just as hard as his face.

"Hold your horses. You'll get your money," Jacob said, "but don't forget about the rest of our deal."

The man narrowed his eyes at Jacob. "As long as you have the money, we'll hold up our end of the bargain."

When Jacob bent down to retrieve the money from his bag, Elizabeth knew this might be her only chance. Summoning every ounce of strength she had, she bolted, racing through the brush as fast as her skirts would allow. Her heart pounded wildly, drowning out the shouts behind her. She didn't dare look back. She just ran, but she wasn't fast enough.

A sharp crack split the air. Elizabeth cried out as a bullet whizzed past her cheek, the sting of its passing nearly knocking her off her feet.

"Stop right there!" Jacob bellowed. Elizabeth risked a glance over her shoulder to find him pointing a gun in her direction, and though she couldn't see his eyes, she had no doubt they would be blazing with the same fury that was evident in his voice. Her breath caught in her throat at the sight of the gun, and she hesitated. She didn't know how good a shot Jacob was, but if his last shot was any indication, she feared he was a good one.

Elizabeth froze in her tracks, chest heaving. As much as she longed to flee, to escape this nightmare, she couldn't risk that he would make good on his threat. She wouldn't do that to Carl or to Emma.

Defeated, she raised her hands in surrender and turned back to face Jacob. He stalked toward her, shoving the gun into his belt before grabbing her arm in a tight grip.

"You'll pay for that," he hissed, his eyes dark with rage. Elizabeth swallowed against the lump in her throat, steeling herself for what was to come.

She had lost this battle, but the war was far from over. Jacob would not break her. Not if she had anything to say about it.

"Looks like you got a feisty one," the other man said, chuckling as they approached. Elizabeth noticed he had a long scar down the side of his face. She wondered briefly how he'd gotten it and then realized she didn't want to know.

"You just take care of your end, and I'll take care of her," Jacob said, squeezing her arms tighter.

The other man held his hands up as in surrender and backed away, still chuckling as he did.

Jacob dragged Elizabeth into the cave and shoved her roughly inside. She stumbled and fell to her knees on the cold, hard ground. Pain erupted in her knees and palms as the tiny rocks cut into her skin, and when the scent of copper hit her nose, she knew she was bleeding.

The cave was pitch black, damp and musty. In addition to the copper, an odd, unpleasant smell lingered in the air that turned her stomach. As her eyes adjusted to the darkness, she began to make out vague shapes in the shadows—

jagged stalactites hanging from the ceiling like sinister teeth, piles of rubble along the walls. An old lantern sat on a crate in the corner, coated in dust and cobwebs.

Panic rose in Elizabeth's chest as the reality of her situation sank in. She had no idea where she was and neither did anyone else. She was trapped. Alone at the mercy of a madman with no one around for miles.

"How did you find me?" she asked, forcing her voice to sound strong. She turned to face Jacob, who stood silhouetted in the entrance of the cave. "And why? Why couldn't you just let me go?"

"I told you that you were mine, and I don't take kindly to losing things I own." Jacob's tone was eerily calm, which only served to heighten her fear. "As for finding you, that was pretty easy once your friend Mary finally started talking."

Elizabeth shook her head. "Mary would never..."

"Not without a little persuading, but once she spilled that you were heading west, I figured you must have gone by train and the good ticket agent was kind enough to tell me which ticket you bought. Following your coach was a little harder, but thankfully you made quite an impression and my money serves as an efficient motivator. I didn't know how you got the money until I arrived here." He shook his head. "You really thought a husband would buy your freedom?"

Rage burned in Elizabeth's stomach, and she curled her hands into fists, wanting nothing more than to pummel

Jacob's smug face but knowing she'd never win. "You better not have laid a hand on Mary."

Jacob chuckled darkly. "As if you care about her. You left her there knowing I would question the girls when you went missing."

"I tried to get her to come with me. She was too brainwashed to leave, too demoralized. She thinks she can't do any better than you, but when I get out of here, I'm going to find Mary and bring her here. At least she'd be free." Elizabeth hadn't thought much about Mary since she'd left, but she did now, and if the woman was still alive, she was going to rescue her. And get her things back.

Jacob laughed, a deep throaty laugh that sent shivers down Elizabeth's spine. "As if you'll be getting away from me again? You've caused me too much trouble already. It's time you learned your lesson."

He took a step toward her and Elizabeth scrambled back against the cave wall, her heart pounding wildly. "Stay away from me!"

Jacob let out a low, sinister chuckle. "There's nowhere to run now. You're mine."

Elizabeth squeezed her eyes shut as panic overwhelmed her, but she had to stay calm. Had to think. There had to be a way out of this. She wasn't going to give up hope. Not yet. Jacob hadn't won, not by a long shot. She would find a way to escape, or die trying.

Then suddenly she heard Carl's words in her head. If she trusted Him, God would see her through this. He'd been talking about the situation in town, but why couldn't God see her through this as well?

God, please help me through this. Give me the strength and the wisdom to get out of this.

Elizabeth opened her eyes and lunged at Jacob, clawing at his face with her fingernails. He let out a roar of anger and pain, grasping her wrists in an iron grip to restrain her.

"You little witch!" he spat, eyes blazing with fury. Blood dripped down his cheek where she had raked her nails across his skin. "You'll pay for that."

He slammed her back against the cave wall, the blow forcing the air from her lungs in a pained gasp. Elizabeth struggled against his grip, kicking out at his shins and stomping on his feet, but he was too strong.

"Enough of this nonsense," Jacob growled. He twisted her arms behind her back and bound her wrists together with a length of rope he produced from his coat pocket. Then he did the same to her ankles.

Elizabeth tugged helplessly at the ropes, her shoulders burning from the strain, but it was no use. She had failed. She was going to die here, alone in this dank, dark cave. No one would find her or even know she was missing until it was too late.

Tears stung at the corners of her eyes but she refused to let them fall. She wouldn't give Jacob the satisfaction of seeing her break down. She had to stay strong, keep fighting, and pray for a miracle. As long as she drew breath, she wouldn't give up hope.

Jacob strode to the mouth of the cave, blocking out the

meager light that filtered in. "I'll be back for you soon," he said with a sneer. "Try to get comfortable."

And with that, he disappeared, leaving Elizabeth alone in the dark, cold cave. The cold slithered around her like a snake, and the darkness enveloped her - a heavy blanket she could not throw off. Blood and tears mingled on her face as despair threatened to overwhelm her. She didn't know how long she would be trapped here or what horrors Jacob had in store for her.

All she knew was that she had to survive. She had to escape, no matter the cost. Her life depended on it.

CHAPTER 22

Carl

Carl had just sat down to dinner when he heard Elizabeth's horse approach the cabin. She was earlier than he thought she'd be which didn't bode well for her having had a good day. With a sigh, he took one bite of the beans and then headed out to help her with the horse, but when he stepped outside, a cold sense of dread filled his chest. Brownie was there, stomping her hooves and throwing her head around, but there was no sign of Elizabeth.

"Elizabeth?" he called as he approached the mare. He didn't think she'd had time to get off the horse and disappear from sight, but the alternative left his throat dry with fear. "Elizabeth?" He scoured the area again, but there was no sign of movement other than from the mare in front of him.

"Easy girl," he said, grabbing her reins in an effort to

calm her down. "What happened out there? Where's Elizabeth?"

The horse couldn't talk, of course, but the fear he saw in the mare's dark eyes was enough to tell him that something bad had happened. He walked the horse to the barn, speaking soothing words as he did even though every bone in his body wanted to race towards town. As soon as her saddle was removed and she was back in her stall though, he mounted his own horse and took off at a gallop for the general store.

He had barely pulled the horse to a stop before he was sliding down and throwing the reins over the post. Then he pushed open the door. "Mr. Brown?"

The elder man looked up from behind the counter at the outburst, his forehead wrinkling in concern. "Mr. Baxter? Is something wrong?"

"You tell me. What happened here this morning and where's Elizabeth?"

"Elizabeth?" The man fumbled with his glasses as they slid down his nose. "She left this morning. Someone cut the fence at the Johnson's, so I told her I had to take down her dress and close her shop until it was cleared up. She wasn't happy, but she said she understood and then she left. I assumed she was returning home. Are you telling me she never made it?"

"That's exactly what I'm telling you. Her horse just returned, spooked as all get out, but Elizabeth wasn't on her."

Mr. Brown's eyes widened. "The horse just returned? But she left hours ago."

Carl didn't wait to hear any more. If Elizabeth had left hours ago and not made it home, something had clearly happened to her. He made a beeline for the sheriff's office.

"Sheriff, we need to assemble a search party."

The sheriff looked up from his desk and blinked at Carl. "A search party for whom?"

"My wife. She's gone missing."

With an exasperated exhale, the sheriff's posture relaxed. "Missing, has she? Well, that's rather convenient after last night's incident. We were just about to ride out to your homestead to bring her in. Now that most of the cattle have been accounted for."

Carl resisted the urge to pound his fist into something. "Elizabeth had nothing to do with what happened at the Johnson's. Once again, she was with me all evening, but she is missing. Mr. Brown said she left this morning, but her horse just came back without her."

This caused the sheriff's eyebrow to lift slightly, but still the man didn't rise from his chair. "Well, perhaps she left town then. Mr. Brown probably warned her that we were going to be coming for her."

"Did you not hear me? Her horse came back without her. If she was leaving town, why wouldn't she take the horse?"

The sheriff leaned back in his chair, clearly nonplussed by this information. "Perhaps she met up with someone who gave her a ride or maybe she just didn't want to add horse thieving to her growing list of crimes. Who knows?

You should count yourself lucky, Mr. Baxter. She could have cleaned you out as well."

Carl gritted his teeth and glared at the man. "Elizabeth is not a thief. Something has happened to her, and if you aren't going to do anything about it, then I guess I'll just have to myself." With that, Carl yanked open the door and stormed back over to his horse. In seconds, he was cracking the reins and galloping toward Jesse Jennings's homestead. He might not be a deputy any longer, but Carl had no doubt the man would help him.

As he rode, Carl's mind spun in circles, imagining Elizabeth cold and afraid, or worse. He couldn't lose her. Not now, not when they'd just started healing again, when he was just beginning to hope for a future together.

When he reached Jesse's homestead, he slid off the horse and raced to the door, pounding on it as he hollered. "Jesse! I need your help. Elizabeth is missing."

The door flew open, and Jesse stood there with Kate behind him, the baby cradled in her arms. Both of them stared at him with alarm. "What happened?"

"Evidently someone broke into Doc's clinic two days ago and the Johnson's farm last night. The sheriff thinks it was Elizabeth, but it wasn't. She went to the store this morning, but never came home. But her horse did. The sheriff thinks she just ran off, but I know something is wrong. Will you help me look for her?"

"Of course he will," Kate said, her eyes pleading with her husband. "I don't believe Elizabeth did any of those things and I know she wouldn't run off like that."

Jesse nodded and grabbed his gun. "Let's go, but we're taking William too."

Carl paused momentarily. He knew Jesse was right. Though he and William Cook weren't on the best terms, the man had been a deputy and a bounty hunter, and he would be an asset in this situation. "Fine, if you think he'll help us, but we have to hurry before it gets dark."

There were probably still a few hours of daylight left, but Carl had no idea which way Elizabeth had gone which meant there was a lot of ground to cover and with only three of them, that would mean riding hard and fast.

"He will." Jesse mounted up on his horse and led the way to William and Emma's homestead. It took only a few minutes for William to agree, and after a brief discussion, they decided the best bet would be to start with the way Elizabeth would ride home. In order for her horse to make it back when she did, Elizabeth couldn't have been too far off the normal path.

"We don't know exactly what we're looking for," William said when they reached the edge of town, "so be looking for anything. Hoof prints, broken branches, pieces of clothing."

Carl glanced up sharply at the last words, but William was right. If Elizabeth had been forced off her horse either accidentally or maliciously, then there was a good chance her dress might have caught on the rough terrain. Though he wanted to push his horse as fast as he possibly could, Carl knew they might miss something if they went too fast, so he sent up a prayer for patience, slowed his horse to a walk, and kept his eyes peeled for anything out of the ordinary.

"What's that?" Jesse asked, pointing to the left as they entered the thick brush just outside of town.

William pulled his horse closer and then dismounted as the small blue item was caught on a stick near the ground. He plucked it up and looked at Carl. "Do you know what color dress Elizabeth was wearing?"

A lump formed in Carl's throat as he stared down at the blue fabric. "It was blue." He remembered because it had brought out the color of her eyes. They had been the color of the sky just before a storm.

"This might be hers then, but which way do we go from here?" William turned in a circle, trying to find anything else to lead them in the right direction.

The men scoured the area, looking for any sign of blood, a struggle, something that would tell them which direction to head, but there was nothing. It was as if Elizabeth had disappeared completely. Suddenly, they heard footsteps approaching in the brush. Each of them froze and reached for their guns, but when the brush parted and Christian Turner stepped through, the men all relaxed.

"Whoa, what are you all doing on my land?" He had one hand on the revolver on his hip, but it was still holstered thankfully. His other hand held a lantern.

Jesse shook his head. "This isn't your land, Christian. It's still part of the town."

"Well, the cave is mine. I been prospecting it for months, so it's mine now."

Carl leaned forward. "There's a cave near here?" How did he not know that? "Have you seen anyone else nearby? My wife, Elizabeth?"

Removing his hand from his gun, Christian scratched his beard thoughtfully. "Can't say I saw a woman exactly. But a fellow came through here in an awful hurry an hour or so ago. He might have come from the direction of the cave. I told him it was my land, but he ignored me. He was acting mighty strange too, so gun or no gun, I'm getting him out of my cave before he steals my gold."

"Did you recognize the man? Notice anything special about him? Was he a local?" Jesse asked.

Christian's forehead wrinkled in thought. "Now that you mention it, I think he did have a scratch or two on his face. Probably got a little too close to the brambles in his hurry. As for him being a local, I don't think so, though I might have seen him in the saloon a few nights ago."

Carl's heart sank. It was possible the man had something to do with Elizabeth, but it was just as likely it was another prospector who'd just happened across the cave. "Was it just the one man?"

Christian nodded. "That I know of, but I brought a second gun just in case." He tapped the rifle slung over his shoulder.

The men exchanged a glance - none of them wanted Christian firing a gun - and then William spoke up. "Can you take us to the cave? We promise we won't touch your gold. In fact, we'll help you clear the man out of your cave."

Christian looked between the three men and sighed. "If

it'll help find this woman of yours and get that man out of my cave then I reckon I could show you the trail, but you better not tell anyone else where my cave is."

The men agreed. None of them were prospectors and they knew Christian well enough to realize there probably wasn't any gold in the cave anyway.

"We better leave the horses here so we can be quieter," Christian said.

Carl hated the idea of leaving the horses. They had no idea what condition Elizabeth might be in, and if she needed medical care, he wanted to be able to get her to the clinic quickly, but the horses would be louder than them approaching on foot, so he reluctantly dismounted and followed the others. His pulse raced as Christian led the way through the brush. Who was this man? And did he have Elizabeth?

When the cave came into view, Christian pointed toward the entrance. "That's it. That's my cave." He paused for a minute as he looked at the men. "Did none of you bring a lantern?"

"We hadn't exactly planned to be searching caves," Carl grumbled.

"Well, here you can take mine. It's dark in that cave, so you'll need it."

Carl's heart seized as he thought about Elizabeth in a dark cave. He wondered if she was scared, hurt. Had the man left her in the dark?

"Alright. We don't know exactly what we're dealing with, so Christian, you wait here. Carl and William and I will go in." The men nodded and Carl fell into line behind Jesse with William bringing up the lead.

Jesse held the lantern high as they entered, and though the lantern cast a dim glow over the cave walls, the interior appeared empty. Then Carl spotted a shadowy figure slumped against the far wall. "Elizabeth!" He ran to her side, dropping to his knees. Her hands and feet were bound, and a nasty bruise marked her cheek, but she was breathing.

"Carl?" Her eyes fluttered open, disbelief and relief warring in her expression. "How did you find me?"

"Never mind that now." He pulled a knife from his boot and cut the ropes binding her wrists and ankles, grimacing at the angry red marks on them. "I'm getting you out of here."

"It's Jacob, the man from my past. He's planning something more, but I don't know exactly what."

Carl's jaw tightened as he helped her up. He didn't know this man, but if he was willing to kidnap Elizabeth, he hated to think about what else he was capable of. "We have to move quickly then." He wrapped an arm around her for support. "Can you walk?"

Elizabeth nodded though he could see the grimace of pain cross her features. "I think so."

Before they reached the entrance of the cave though, they were met with a venomous glare the barrel of a gun pointed right at them. "I don't know who you are, but it looks like you're trying to steal what I rightfully own."

Red hot anger fueled through Carl, and he stepped in front of Elizabeth. "Elizabeth is not property to be owned, and considering she's my wife, it appears that you are the thief here."

Jacob's eyes shifted to Elizabeth. "So this is the husband." He shook his head. "No matter. Once you're dead, she'll be free to marry me as she should have in the beginning. Now, put your guns down on the ground."

Carl's gun was in his holster where he'd placed it in order to free Elizabeth. He'd never get it drawn before Jacob fired. Jesse had his gun drawn but also the lantern in his other hand which might impede his shot. Only William had a good shot, and though Carl knew he was a quick shot, he wondered if it would be quick enough. He sneaked a glance at William, but before the man could decide to fire or lower his weapon, there was a loud thud and Jacob crumpled to the floor.

Carl looked back to the entrance to see Christian there, holding a large iron prospecting pan and staring down at the man. "I told him this was my cave."

"Quick, before he wakes up," Jesse hollered. William dashed out of the cave and returned a few moments later with a length of rope. Then he tied up Jacob's hands and feet.

"Let's get him to the sheriff and see if we can figure out what else he has planned." William turned to Elizabeth. "Can you tell us anything more?"

Elizabeth mashed her lips together as she thought. "There was another man. He's the one who carried me here. He had long scraggly hair, cold eyes, and a scar across his face." She motioned the size and position on her own face.

Jesse and William exchanged glances. "That could be one of the outlaws the sheriff has been after," Jesse said. "We better hurry."

Jesse and William carried Jacob to William's horse while Carl followed behind with Elizabeth. The thought of taking her back into town when people were still against her made him sick to his stomach, but she needed to be looked at. As if sensing his concern, she placed a hand on his arm.

"It's okay. I'll be alright. I'm more worried about what Jacob has planned."

He planted a quick kiss on her forehead, careful to avoid the bruises. "Don't worry. They'll figure it out."

As the men loaded up, Carl turned back to Christian who had followed them back to the horses. "Are you coming?"

Christian shook his head. "Nope, I got more digging to do in my cave. You remember what I said though. Don't be telling nobody where it is."

Carl smiled at the man. "Don't worry. Your secret is safe with us." Carl just hoped he could keep Elizabeth as safe as Christian's secret.

CHAPTER 23
Elizabeth

"Oh my gosh, what happened?" Emma asked as Carl helped Elizabeth into the clinic.

"A man from my past who didn't like that I left him tried to take me back," Elizabeth said grimly, wincing as Carl helped her to the bed. "And speaking of Jacob," she said, turning to Carl, "you better go see if you can help the men figure out what else he has planned."

"I can't leave you," he said, clasping her hand.

"Yes, you can. You don't know Jacob. He's maniacal, and if he's working with an outlaw, then he has something big planned. You have to find out what it is."

"Go," Emma said. "I will take good care of Elizabeth."

Carl chewed on his lip but finally nodded. "I'll be back as soon as I can."

As soon as he was gone, Emma began examining Elizabeth. "Can you tell me where it hurts?"

Elizabeth held out her palms. "These for sure. Plus my

knees. He pushed me to the ground, so my hip is sore. Plus, I fell off the horse, hit my backside and my head. I think they used something to spook her."

"Okay, let's start with cleaning your hands and knees first." Emma grabbed a piece of cloth and dipped it in the water bowl, but as soon as she wiped it across Elizabeth's palms, she gasped. Emma's features folded in sympathy. "Sorry, this is going to hurt for a bit."

Elizabeth nodded and pressed her lips together. Slowly, the pain began to ease in her palms though they were still red and angry. Her knees came next but before Emma could assess the other issues from the fall, a bell began to ring out. Elizabeth's eyes snapped up. "What is that?"

Emma's eyes were wide with fear. "That's the town bell. They only ring it when danger is affecting the whole town. We have to lock the door and hide."

"Hide? But what if this is about Jacob? Shouldn't we try to help?"

"And get ourselves killed? No; we wait."

Elizabeth looked desperately toward the door which Emma was locking. "But Carl is out there, William..."

The lock clicked and Emma turned. "William is a great shot, and the men will protect us, whatever Jacob is planning. Now, come on, we have to get behind some shelter." She hurried back across the room and grabbed Elizabeth's hand, pulling her to the floor behind the bed. Then she turned it over as if to protect them.

"What do we do now?" Elizabeth asked.

Emma looked at her and grabbed her hand. "Now, we pray."

Elizabeth took a deep breath and closed her eyes. As Emma began to pray, Elizabeth joined in. "Lord, please keep the men safe. Keep the town safe." The sound of gunshots caused Elizabeth to jump. She tightened her grip on Emma's hands. "Please keep us safe."

There were a few more shots and then the gunfire stopped. Elizabeth's eyes opened and she met Emma's gaze. "Is it over? Can we go find them?"

Emma shook her head. "Not yet. We have to be sure."

Elizabeth nodded, but her heart pounded in her chest. How was she supposed to sit here, not knowing if Carl was okay out there? It was her fault that Jacob had come to Sage Creek, after all.

A knock at the door caused her to jump, but then her heart lifted when she heard the voice on the other side. "Elizabeth? Emma? Are you two okay in there?"

"Carl? We're fine." She turned to Emma. "We have to open the door."

Emma nodded. "You stay here. I'll make sure it's really safe."

Elizabeth watched from around the corner of the bed as Emma made her way to the windows, looked outside, and then opened the door.

Carl rushed in first, crossing the room to pick up Elizabeth as she tried to stand. Before he threw his arms around her and pulled her to his chest, she saw William envelop Emma in a similar gesture. Her heart swelled as she realized

Carl had run to her and not to Emma. She knew at that moment that whatever had been between them was gone now, and the wall of protection she'd placed around her heart crumbled. She'd finally found a man she could love.

"What happened out there?" she asked. "We heard gunfire."

Carl pulled back so he could look into her face. "We managed to get Jacob to tell us what he'd done. Evidently, he'd found a band of outlaws and convinced them to attack the town in exchange for money. Who knows if he would have actually paid them, but when they rode into town and saw we had Jacob in custody, it only took a few warning shots to get them to leave. It's over, Elizabeth. Jacob confessed to breaking into the clinic and cutting the Johnson's fence as well. He was hoping to turn the town against you so you would leave."

"And he almost succeeded." She pressed her lips together, hope filling her for the first time in ages, but could it really be that easy? Would the townspeople finally accept her?

"Yes, he did, but I promise he will never hurt you again. The sheriff is sending him to the Huntsville prison."

"And the town? Do you think they'll finally accept me?"

"I know they will. They're good people at heart."

Good people… "Carl, I need to ask a favor of you." It was a lot to ask, but she knew she wouldn't be truly happy until she tried.

"What is it?" he asked and Elizabeth took a deep breath.

CHAPTER 24
Elizabeth

Elizabeth squeezed Carl's hand and led him toward the saloon. She couldn't believe that he'd agreed to return to Chicago with her, but she was grateful. Their first stop had been the bank where they'd presented their marriage certificate and received a key for the storage area holding her belongings the bank hadn't sold. Then they'd procured transfer of the belongings by train, and while she was certain she would have been able to do all of this alone, it was certainly both easier and more enjoyable with her husband by her side. Now, there was just one thing left to do.

When they reached the swinging doors, Elizabeth's throat dried up. She had hoped to never see this place again, yet here she was, walking back into it. Voluntarily. But it was for a good cause. She had to convince her friend to come with them; she had to at least try.

"Hey, it will be alright," Carl whispered in her ear at her hesitation.

She gave him a tight smile. "I know, but it doesn't make it any easier."

"I'm right here with you."

Nodding, Elizabeth took a deep breath and pushed open the doors. Cigar smoke clouded the air in the dim establishment, and the sound of clanking glasses and conversation reverberated around the room and assaulted her ears. She wasn't used to this environment anymore and it was overwhelming.

"Elizabeth? Is that you?"

She turned her head to the left, trying to find the voice of the woman who'd spoken. It took her a moment, but then she found Mary's face, and she smiled. "Mary, you're still here." As she got closer though, Elizabeth's smile faltered. Not only did the woman look older, but there were bruises on her face, and anger surged through Elizabeth.

Mary glanced over at the bar before hurrying toward Elizabeth. Her eyes were filled with fear and sadness. "I'm so sorry, Elizabeth. I tried to be strong, but I wasn't."

Elizabeth wanted to pull the woman into a hug, but she didn't think Mary would allow that here, so instead she simply shook her head. "It's okay. I understand."

"But how can you not be mad? You were supposed to get out of here, and now you're back and Jacob is probably never going to give you a chance to escape again."

Elizabeth grabbed her friend's hands. "Jacob came after me, but he's not why I'm here. I came back for you."

Mary's brows furrowed in surprise, and she glanced around again. Elizabeth followed her gaze but knew the woman was looking for Luther. "But I don't understand. If he came after you, how did you get away?"

Elizabeth smiled and glanced back at Carl. "This is my husband, Carl Baxter. He saved me and then he and his friends made sure Jacob was arrested. He's in prison, Mary. He's not getting out anytime soon. I know you said you couldn't leave here, but this is no place for you." She squeezed Mary's hands. "Come back with us. Come to Sage Creek. I have a dress shop that I'm opening and a job for you. You won't have to do saloon work any longer."

"A dress shop? But I don't know the first thing about working in a dress shop, Elizabeth."

"But you will. You sew and you're a quick learner. I know it. Please, Mary. I can't bear the thought of leaving you here."

Mary chewed on her lip and glanced over at the bar again. "You're sure Jacob is in prison?"

"Yes ma'am," Carl said, stepping toward them. "He's in the Huntsville prison and won't be getting out anytime soon."

"But what about a place to live?" She dropped her eyes, humiliation covering her face. "I don't have much money saved up."

Elizabeth smiled at Carl. Now that they were sharing the bedroom, he'd agreed to let Mary take their couch until he could build an extra room on their cabin. Eventually that room would be for children, but that was in the future.

"You'll stay with us until you can afford a place on your own or until you find a nice man to marry." Though she wouldn't say it aloud, Elizabeth could see Mary and Mr. Brown together. He was about the right age, a widower, and Elizabeth knew he would treat her friend right. "Please, Mary, there's nothing left for you here. When they find out Jacob is in prison, this place might even close, and even if it doesn't, do you want to continue working for Luther?"

Mary looked back once more at the bar and then shook her head. "No, I definitely do not. Give me a minute to grab my things."

As Mary dashed up the stairs, Elizabeth turned to Carl and grabbed his hands. "Thank you. For coming with me and for letting Mary return with us."

Carl pulled her to his chest and kissed the top of her head, careful to avoid the fading bruise on her forehead. "I'm happy to help. No woman should be forced to work in a place like this."

Mary returned a few moments later, a bag clasped in her hands and a large smile on her face. "I guess I'm ready."

Elizabeth wrapped an arm around her friend's shoulder and led her toward the door, but before they were able to step into the sunlight, Luther stepped into their path.

"Well, Jacob is going to be mighty pleased to see that you've returned," he said, his eyes scanning Elizabeth before turning to Mary. "And where do you think you're going?"

Carl stepped in front of the women. "Jacob is in prison and these women are going with me, so unless you'd like to join your former boss, I suggest you step aside."

Elizabeth held her breath as she watched Luther size up Carl. Luther was ruthless, but evidently something in Carl's eyes warned the man he was telling the truth. After a moment, Luther snorted in disgust and stepped aside. "Good riddance then. You were getting too old to be useful anyway."

Elizabeth felt Mary's shoulders sag, and she whispered to her friend. "Don't listen to him. He's just salty that you're moving on to something better."

Mary chuckled sadly. "He's not wrong though. I am getting too old to be useful."

"Not to me. You're going to be more help for me than you know." Elizabeth had only picked up one other client besides Emma, but she had faith that more would come and that God would provide.

Epilogue ~ Elizabeth
THREE MONTHS LATER

Elizabeth smiled as she watched Mary dance with Mr. Brown across the room. Though she'd been timid at first, she'd settled into Sage Creek almost effortlessly.

"They make a cute couple," Carl said, coming up behind her and wrapping his arms around her.

She turned to him and smiled. "Yes, they do. I had a feeling they would hit it off, but even I didn't expect it to happen this quickly."

Mary and Mr. Brown had seemed to share an instant attraction the moment Elizabeth introduced the two, and though they had just started courting, she had no doubt that he would propose soon.

"I guess it's a good thing it did though," Carl said as he lowered his hands to the small baby bump that was just starting to be noticeable. "We're going to need that room back soon."

"There's still plenty of time," she said, shaking her head. "At least another seven months."

"It will be here before you know it. Have you thought about what you are going to do about the business then?"

Elizabeth sighed and nodded. She was looking forward to this baby, more than anything, but she was a little sad that she'd finally achieved her dream and now it would have to change. "I have. As long as Mary is comfortable running the store, she can take orders for me and I can sew at home. I'll probably have to either move lessons there as well or limit when I offer them, but I think I can make both work."

He turned her around so that she was facing him. "I have no doubt you can. You are an amazing woman, and I told you the town would come around."

Elizabeth chuckled. "Yes, well, Rebecca apologizing had a lot to do with that. That and catching the real culprit."

Rebecca hadn't been dying to apologize, but after Jacob was sent to prison and the sheriff and deputy had given Elizabeth a public pardon, she'd needed to in order to save face. The gossip around town had been that she'd been jealous of Carl and Elizabeth and had shared Emma and Carl's history in an effort to break them up. Though it had been petty, Elizabeth could almost understand the girl's frustration. There were so few eligible women in town that it had to be a slap in the face when the men looked elsewhere for a wife. She still didn't trust Rebecca, but she prayed that God would soften her heart toward the woman and send the right man for her soon.

"Speaking of that, have you heard that Deputy Masterson and Rebecca are courting?" Carl asked.

"Deputy Masterson?"

Carl chuckled. "Yep. I guess it makes sense. Rebecca was Pauline's best friend. She's known James forever, and if you ask me, the two kind of deserve each other."

Elizabeth wasn't sure she wanted Rebecca married to a deputy. The woman didn't need any more power, but she hoped the two would find happiness. Maybe love would soften them both.

"But, let's not talk any more about them tonight," Carl said as if reading her mind. "I want to spend tonight dancing with my wife and watching her enjoy the fruits of her labor."

As Carl led her to the dance floor, Elizabeth realized he was right. Though not every woman was wearing a dress she'd made, several were, and others were wearing ones they'd added lace or some decoration to during lessons with Elizabeth. Nearly every dress in the room had been influenced by her in some way and that did feel good, but even more than that, seeing the smiles on the faces of the women felt even better.

She wrapped her arms around Carl's neck and smiled up at him. This might not be the life she'd imagined for herself, but that was okay because it was even better. "I love you, Carl."

He grinned down at her and pulled her closer. "And I love you."

The End!

There's more in store for Sage Creek, but I'd love to know who you'd like the next story about. Would you like to read about Mary, Rebecca, Sarah, or Carrie? Click **this link** to vote and look for the next book soon.

And would you please leave a review at your retailer. Just a few words is all you need to say.

CHAPTER 25
Author's Note

First off, let me say how glad I am that you read this book. It has taken me a while to return to Sage Creek, but when the world gets a little crazy, I find myself enjoying this jump to the past when it was a little simpler and a little saner.

I hope you enjoyed this book. If you did, would you do me a favor? Please leave a review at your retailer. It really helps. It doesn't have to be long - just a few words to help other readers know what they're getting.

I'd love to hear from you, not only about this story, but about the characters or stories you'd like read in the future. I'm always looking for new ideas and if I use one of your characters or stories, I'll send you a free ebook and paperback of the book with a special dedication. Write to me at loranahoopes@gmail.com. And if you'd like to see what's coming next, be sure to stop by authorloranahoopes.com

I also have a weekly newsletter that contains many wonderful things like pictures of my adorable children, chances to win awesome prizes, new releases and sales I might be holding, great books from other authors, and anything else that strikes my fancy and that I think you would enjoy. I'll even send you the first chapter of my newest (maybe not even released yet) book if you'd like to sign up.

Even better, I solemnly swear to only send out one news-letter a week (usually on Tuesday unless life gets in the way which with three kids it usually does). I will not spam you, sell your email address to solicitors or anyone else, or any of those other terrible things.

This series will be continued, but for now, would you like to meet some characters for a new series.

Prayers and blessings,
   Lorana

CHAPTER 26
Not ready to say Goodbye yet?

S age Creek is up and coming, and I have more stories for it. Tell me who you want to read about next

Carrie - The younger sister of Emma who was sweet on a boy in A Second Chance at Love. Does he return her feelings?

Sarah - The daughter of the cafe owners who befriends Kate in An Unexpected Love?

Rebecca - The woman who seems to have a jealous streak and has been a villain but might find the perfect man for her?

Mary - The older woman Elizabeth brought back from Chicago. Could she find a second chance with Mr. Brown?

Vote for your favorite using this link and look for the next book soon.

CHAPTER 27
A Free Story For You

Enjoyed this story? Not ready to quit reading yet? If you sign up for my newsletter, you will receive The Billionaire's Impromptu Bet right away as my thank you gift for choosing to hang out with me.

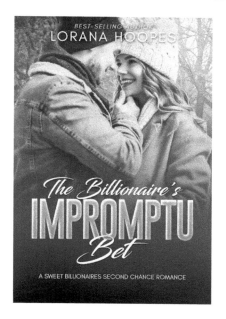

The Billionaire's Impromptu Bet

A SWAT officer. A bored billionaire heiress. A bet that could change everything....

Read on for a taste of The Billionaire's Impromptu Bet....

CHAPTER 28
The Billionaire's Impromptu Bet Preview

Brie Carter fell back spread eagle on her queen-sized canopy bed sending her blond hair fanning out behind her. With a large sigh, she uttered, "I'm bored."

"How can you be bored? You have like millions of dollars." Her friend, Ariel, plopped down in a seated position on the bed beside her and flicked her raven hair off her shoulder. "You want to go shopping? I hear Tiffany's is having a special right now."

Brie rolled her eyes. Shopping? Where was the excitement in that? With her three platinum cards, she could go shopping whenever she wanted. "No, I'm bored with shopping too. I have everything. I want to do something exciting. Something we don't normally do."

Brie enjoyed being rich. She loved the unlimited credit cards at her disposal, the constant apparel of new clothes, and of course the penthouse apartment her father paid for, but lately, she longed for something more fulfilling.

Ariel's hazel eyes widened. "I know. There's a new bar down on Franklin Street. Why don't we go play a little game?"

Brie sat up, intrigued at the secrecy and the twinkle in Ariel's eyes. "What kind of game?"

"A betting game. You let me pick out any man in the place. Then you try to get him to propose to you."

Brie wrinkled her nose. "But I don't want to get married." She loved her freedom and didn't want to share her penthouse with anyone, especially some man.

"You don't marry him, silly. You just get him to propose."

Brie bit her lip as she thought. It had been awhile since her last relationship and having a man dote on her for a month might be interesting, but…. "I don't know. It doesn't seem very nice."

"How about I sweeten the pot? If you win, I'll set you up on a date with my brother."

Brie cocked her head. Was she serious? The only thing Brie couldn't seem to buy in the world was the affection of Ariel's very handsome, very wealthy, brother. He was a movie star, just the kind of person Brie could consider marrying in the future. She'd had a crush on him as long as she and Ariel had been friends, but he'd always seen her as just that, his little sister's friend. "I thought you didn't want me dating your brother."

"I don't." Ariel shrugged. "But he's between girlfriends right now, and I know you've wanted it for ages. If you win this bet, I'll set you up. I can't guarantee any more than one date though. The rest will be up to you."

Brie wasn't worried about that. Charm she possessed in abundance. She simply needed some alone time with him, and she was certain she'd be able to convince him they were meant to be together. "All right. You've got a deal."

Ariel smiled. "Perfect. Let's get you changed then and see who the lucky man will be.

A tiny tug pulled on Brie's heart that this still wasn't right, but she dismissed it. This was simply a means to an end, and he'd never have to know.

Jesse Calhoun relaxed as the rhythmic thudding of the speed bag reached his ears. Though he loved his job, it was stressful being the SWAT sniper. He hated having to take human lives and today had been especially rough. The team had been called out to a drug bust, and Jesse was forced to return fire at three hostiles. He didn't care that they fired at his team and himself first. Taking a life was always hard, and every one of them haunted his dreams.

"You gonna bust that one too?" His co-worker Brendan appeared by his side. Brendan was the opposite of Jesse in nearly every way. Where Jesse's hair was a dark copper, Brendan's was nearly black. Jesse sported paler skin and a dusting of freckles across his nose, but Brendan's skin was naturally dark and freckle free.

Jesse flashed a crooked grin, but kept his eyes on the small, swinging black bag. The speed bag was his way to release, but a few times he had started hitting while still too keyed up and he had ruptured the bag. Okay, five times, but who was counting really? Besides, it was a better way to calm his nerves than other things he could choose. Drinking, fights, gambling, women.

"Nah, I think this one will last a little longer." His shoulders began to burn, and he gave the bag another few punches for good measure before dropping his arms and letting it swing to a stop. "See? It lives to be hit at least another day." Every once in a while, Jesse missed training the way he used to. Before he joined the force, he had been an amateur boxer, on his way to being a pro, but a shoulder injury had delayed his training and forced him to consider something else. It had eventually healed, but by then he had lost his edge.

"Hey, why don't you come drink with us?" Brendan clapped a hand on Jesse's shoulder as they headed into the locker room.

"You know I don't drink." Jesse often felt like the outsider of the team. While half of the six-man team was married, the other half found solace in empty bottles and meaningless relationships. Jesse understood that - their job was such that they never knew if they would come home night after night - but he still couldn't partake.

Brendan opened his locker and pulled out a clean shirt.

He peeled off his current one and added deodorant before tugging on the new one. "You don't have to drink. Look, I won't drink either. Just come and hang out with us. You have no one waiting for you at home."

That wasn't entirely true. Jesse had Bugsy, his Boston Terrier, but he understood Brendan's point. Most days, Jesse went home, fed Bugsy, made dinner, and fell asleep watching TV on the couch. It wasn't much of a life. "All right, I'll go, but I'm not drinking."

Brendan's lips pulled back to reveal his perfectly white teeth. He bragged about them, but Jesse knew they were veneers. "That's the spirit. Hurry up and change. We don't want to leave the rest of the team waiting."

"Is everyone coming?" Jesse pulled out his shower necessities. Brendan might feel comfortable going out with just a new application of deodorant, but Jesse needed to wash more than just dirt and sweat off. He needed to wash the sound of the bullets and the sight of lifeless bodies from his mind.

"Yeah, Pat's wife is pregnant again and demanding some crazy food concoctions. Pat agreed to pick them up if she let him have an hour. Cam and Jared's wives are having a girls' night, so the whole gang can be together. It will be nice to hang out when we aren't worried about being shot at."

"Fine. Give me ten minutes. Unlike you, I like to clean up before I go out."

Brendan smirked. "I've never had any complaints. Besides, do you know how long it takes me to get my hair like this?"

Jesse shook his head as he walked into the shower, but he knew it was true. Brendan had rugged good looks and muscles to match. He rarely had a hard time finding a woman. Jesse on the other hand hadn't dated anyone in the last few months. It wasn't that he hadn't been looking, but he was quieter than his teammates. And he wasn't looking for right now. He was looking for forever. He just hadn't found it yet.

Click here to continue reading The Billionaire's Impromptu Bet.

The Story Doesn't End!

You've met a few people and fallen in love....

I bet you're wondering how you can meet everyone else.

Star Lake Series:

Sealed with a Kiss: Meet the quirky cast of Star Lake and find out if Max and Layla will ever find love.

When Love Returns: Return to Star Lake to hear Presley's story and find out if she gets the second chance with her first love.

Once Upon a Star: Continue the journey when aspiring actress Audrey returns home with a baby. Will Blake finally get the nerve to share his feelings with her?

Love Conquers All: Meet Lanie Perkins Hall who never imagined being divorced at thirty or falling for an old friend, but will his secrets keep them apart?

The Star Lake Collection: Get the latter three stories in one place. Series will include book 1 when it releases around November 2020.

Patriot Peak:

Her Second Chance: When a ghost from Merribeth's past threatens her son, nothing is more important than saving the people that Chance can't keep out of his heart.

Her First Love: A veteran who wants to settle down and start a family. A woman with a secret that could destroy everything.

Her Saving Grace: When Dougie finds out something about the man who's stepped into Holly's life, should he tell her or keep it to himself?

The Heartbeats Series:

Where It All Began: Sandra Baker finds forgiveness and healing even after making a horrible choice.

The Power of Prayer: Will Callie Green find true love or be defined by her mistake?

When Hearts Collide: When Amanda Adams goes to college, she finds a world she was not ready for. But will she also find true love?

A Past Forgiven: Jess Peterson has lived a life of abuse and lost her self worth, but when she finds herself pregnant, will she find new hope?

The Heartbeats Collection: Grab all four Heartbeats novels in one collection

Sweet Billionaires Series:

The Billionaire's Impromptu Bet: Can a spoiled rich girl change when a bet turns to love?

The Billionaire's Secret: Can a playboy settle down when he finds out he has a daughter who needs him?

A Brush with a Billionaire: What happens when a stuck up actor lands in a small town and needs help from a female mechanic?

The Billionaire's Christmas Miracle: A twist on a Cinderella story when a billionaire meets a woman who doesn't belong at the ball.

The Billionaire's Cowboy Groom: Will one night six years ago keep Carrie from finding true love?

The Cowboy Billionaire: Can a small town soften the heart of the man sent to buy her ranch?

The Billionaire's Bliss: This collection contains The Billionaire's Secret, The Billionaire's Christmas Miracle, and The Billionaire's Cowboy Groom

Sweet Billionaire's Collection Two: This collection contains The Billionaire's Impromptu Bet, A Brush with a Billionaire, and The Cowboy Billionaire

The Lawkeeper Series:

An Unexpected Love When the man she agreed to marry turns out to have a dark past, will Kate have to return home or will she find love with her rescuer in this historical fiction?

A Second Chance at Love Can a bounty hunter and a widow find love together in this historical fiction?

An Unforgettable Love: Carl wants to find love and advertises for a mail-order bride. Elizabeth answers to get away from her situation, but can she ever really escape?

Lawfully Redeemed: What happens when a K9 cop falls for the brother of her suspect? Contemporary romance.

The Lawkeeper Collection: Get all four books in one collection

The Are You Listening Series:

The Still Small Voice: Will Jordan listen to God's prompting in this speculative fiction?

A Spark in the Darkness Will Jordan be able to help Raven before the rapture occurs?

The Beginning of the End: After the believers disappear, Raven is left trying to spread the word of God, but a pandemic threatens her progress.

Faith Over Fear: The stunning conclusion to the series.

Are You Listening Collection: All four books in one collection

Blushing Brides Series:

The Cowboy's Reality Bride: He's agreed to be the bachelor on a reality dating show, but what happens when he falls for a woman who's not one of the contestants?

The Reality Bride's Baby: Laney wants nothing more than a baby, but when she starts feeling dizzy is it pregnancy or something more serious?

The Producer's Unlikely Bride: What happens when a producer and an author agree to a fake relationship?

Ava's Blessing in Disguise: Five years after marriage, Ava faces a mysterious illness that threatens to ruin her career. Will she find out what it is?

The Soldier's Steadfast Bride: It was just a pretend pact between children. Wasn't it?

Blushing Brides Collection: The collection of all three novels and the two epilogues

The Men of Fire Beach

Fire Games: Cassidy returns home from Who Wants to Marry a Cowboy to find obsessive letters from a fan. The cop assigned to help her wants to get back to his case, but what she sees at a fire may just be the key he's looking for.

Lost Memories and New Beginnings: A doctor, a patient with no memory, the men out to get her. Can he keep her safe when he doesn't know who he's looking for?

When Questions Abound: A Companion story to Lost Memories. Told from Detective Graves' point of view.

Never Forget the Past: Fireman Bubba must confront his past in order to clear his name and save lives.

Love on the Run: Graham is forced into lockdown with one of his employees. Will he be able to save her from her ex and will she steal his heart?

Secrets and Suspense: Cara Hunter is hiding something about her military past. When she's suspected of murder, will she be able to convince Cole she's the victim?

Rescue My Heart: Al's sister has gone missing. Will she find her in time?

Safe in My Arms: Ivy finds a baby abandoned on the side of the road. Can she keep the baby safe and will she find love along the way?

In the Light of Day Deacon thought he'd left his past behind him, but when she calls and believes she's in danger, will he help her?

In the Dark of Night - Dr. Young has gone missing. Where is he and what happened to him?

The Men of Fire Beach Collection: Books 1-3

The Men of Fire Beach Collection 2: Books 4-6 Coming soon!

Texas Tornadoes

Defending My Heart: Forced to confront his past, Emmitt finds news that will change his life.

Run With My Heart: Sentenced to community service, Tucker finds himself falling for the manager.

Love on the Line: Blaine has hired Kenzi to redo his cabin, but what happens when she finds his darkest secret?

Touchdown on Love: When Mason's injury throws him together with ex-girlfriend, will sparks fly again?

Second Chance Reception: Jefferson is hiding something. When he falls for the team cook, will he let her in?

A Divine Interception: Can Carter and April find love?

Texas Tornadoes Collection 1: Contains books 1-3

Texas Tornadoes Collection 2: Contains books 4-6

Small Town Short Stories

Small Town Dreams

Small Town Second Chances

Small Town Rivals

Small Town Life

Life in a Small Town: All four stories in one collection

Stand Alones:

Love Renewed: This books is part of the multi author second chance series. When fate reunites high school sweethearts separated by life's choices, can they find a second chance at love at a snowy lodge amid a little mystery?

Her children's early reader chapter book series:
    The Wishing Stone #1: Dangerous Dinosaur
    The Wishing Stone #2: Dragon Dilemma
    The Wishing Stone #3: Mesmerizing Mermaids
    The Wishing Stone #4: Pyramid Puzzle
    The Wishing Stone: Mary's Miracle
    The Wishing Stone Collection
    To see a list of all her books

authorloranahoopes.org
loranahoopes@gmail.com

About The Author

Lorana Hoopes is an inspirational author originally from Texas but now living in the PNW with her husband and three children. When not writing, she can be seen kick-boxing at the gym, singing, or acting on stage. One day, she hopes to retire from teaching and write full time.

9 798223 681915